FOR OUR PLANET

(A Cautionary Tale)

By

Debbie Bailey

Dedications:

Fred Glasheen and Maryrose Markham

Thank you for your support and patience, Fred.

Maryrose, you were the best sounding board for this book that came to me in dreams.

I Love You Both

INTRODUCTION:

For Our Planet is a work of fiction, but with global viruses, widespread unemployment, racial unrest, the weakening of Democracies around the world, and climate change all bearing down upon the Earth, I view it as one possible radical outcome of our not-so-distant future.

There is a Protagonist in this story, and her name is Brea. She is 17, smart, curious, brave, but she is no hero. There are no heroes in this story except a couple of people in small but significant ways. If you are looking for a Dystopian tale with a resistance movement, you will be met instead with an unexpected adventure. This will lead Brea and one of her best friends, Dillin, on a journey that changes their lives, but not their circumstances.

This is: For Our Planet.

PART ONE

THE NEIGHBORHOOD

Chapter One

Brea woke up with feelings of giddiness and anticipation, and carefully dressed in her official Gaming outfit. She put on her creased black pants, black socks, black patent leather shoes, long sleeved white blouse, and black vest. She carefully put up her blonde hair in a bun, and styled it with wistful bangs touching her eyebrows, and long thin rings of hair around the edge of her face. This made her green eyes stand out more. Brea stood back and was pleased with her appearance. It was Promotion Day in The Neighborhood, and she wanted to look her best. Today she had another opportunity to be Promoted by The Elites and be a permanent member of her Specialty: Gaming. If chosen, she would travel to any number of gorgeous destinations around the world. Since turning sixteen last year, she had been eligible, but did not get promoted. It had been exceedingly disappointing because Brea was so highly ranked in the Gaming field.

There was no area in Gaming that she was not proficient. Brea could run any poker game, blackjack table, roulette wheel, pia gow, craps, baccarat table, dice, or run any bridge or chess tournament with ease. She could spot a counter, a splitter, a colluder, a card replacer, or any number of cheats within seconds. Brea had finished her basic schooling as all children did by ten years of age. Then joined her classmates in being pretend players for two years before moving on to her three years of professional training. This was where she discovered the new words of currency and money. The Elites used this currency to play these games, and she knew how to change currency to chips faster than anyone else in her class.

Once in a while, a student didn't possess the dexterity in their fingers, the quickness of math, or the attention span to become a Gamer. This was not the case with Brea. On occasion, Coach Fernsbee would ask her to help out in class when an Assistant Coach was ill. This year Brea was ranked number one. Once any student was ranked in the top ten, they were given the title of a Gaming Master. She was ranked above every eighteen year old and, in her mind, this added to her expectation of being promoted today.

She was also in the same class as her two best friends, Lindy and Dillin. They had been friends since kindergarten, and they too were in the top ten, and were Gaming Masters. She never considered them competition except on Promotion Day but would never begrudge them their promotion over her. In fact, once promoted, you never saw those students again. They went off to live their exciting new lives, leaving friends and family behind for good. This was just the way things worked, and everyone accepted it.

If you reached the age of 18 and were not promoted, there were three spots in The Neighborhood left to be assigned. There was Assistant Coach, a teacher of the children 4 to 10 years of age, or a parent. Being picked as a parent was the least desirable to Brea. She had no desire to marry or have children because it seemed to her the dullest of all occupations. Once she reached the age of acquiring fertility, she had been drinking her special vitamins along with every girl in The Neighborhood to avoid becoming with child. If a girl was picked to be a mother, she married and stopped drinking it until she gave birth to two healthy children, and then went back to drinking the concoction. Two children was the maximum per family, and it did not matter if they were both girls or boys. Brea realized a small percentage of each generation was to carry on the populous, but she was determined not to be among them.

She went to say goodbye to her little brother Sami, and he wished her good fortune. Brea did not expect anything more than this from him. Sami was nine and recoiled from hugging their own mom. When she went to her mother, she had a robotic like hug to give her daughter, and just said, "Goodbye." Her next stop was the third floor of her Grandma's. She passed her Aunt and Uncle's floor all together. They weren't that close, but she loved her father's mother very much. Brea's dad had been taken away when she was very young, just after Sami's birth, and this had put an unspoken strain on the entire family. She ignored it by keeping away from her Aunt and Uncle.

It was a privilege in her mind that her father was a part of The Elites as a Doctor and couldn't understand her family's problem with it. Her grandma didn't seem to mind, and that's all that mattered to Brea. When she entered her grandma's room, as always, she was sitting in her recliner and wearing her Headgear but took it off when she saw her granddaughter. They embraced each other tightly, and when Brea sat back on her heels, she saw tears in her Grandma's eyes.

"Please, don't cry."

"I can't help it, child," replied her grandma, "You are the dearest thing in the world to me."

"Grandma! Be happy for me! I might be a part of The Elites in a few hours," said Brea with real excitement in her voice.

"Okay, Sweetie, how's this? I will either never see you again, and wish you Good Fortune, or I'll see you in a couple of hours."

"Well, that sounds just beautiful to me," replied Brea.

They hugged, once more, and then her Grandma put back on her Headgear. All the Grandparents in The Neighborhood had Headgear, but no one ever discussed what it was. Her Grandma only told her that this device made her: Feel Good. And that was that. Once she sneaked and tried on her grandma's Headgear, but it wouldn't work for Brea. It was just like Brea's personal screen in her special chair only worked for her.

When she was done saying her goodbyes, she went straight down to the first floor with nothing said even to her cousins on the second floor. There was no point. Her Father was passed the age of being picked when he was taken. He was a husband, a dad, and it caused a rift in the family. Brea was happy for her dad. He was an Elite. Even those in The Neighborhood knew that Doctors, Nurses, and Scientists could do anything they wanted, and this gave her pride in her father. She did not understand anyone's pain, except a bit of her mom's. To lose your spouse must be a hardship, but since Brea had a laser-like focus on other things she did not fully sympathize with her mom's pain, either. Brea's sole goal was to be picked by and join The Elites.

Chapter Two

She went to the elevator and stepped inside. There were three floors beneath their home. The first floor was the grocery store. In there, the people that belonged to The Gaming part of The Neighborhood did their shopping for food and other necessities. They brought their glass milk bottles to be exchanged from empty to full, and all other manner of household items. This included their clothes and shoes that were picked up or picked out there. A family simply chose what they wanted, and it was supplied to them. On the second floor was the Child Learning School. There the children spent the years from 4 to 10 learning the basics of reading, writing, math, basic science, languages, etiquette, and physical exercise. On the third floor was the Specialty of Gaming.

Underneath the buttons of floors were five letters running across the length of the panel. D for Dining, M for Music and Art, A for Athletics, H for Horticulture, and G for Gaming. These were necessary to swiftly take them to other parts of The Neighborhood. These events took place every 3 months and were called: The Socials. They would visit a different part, intermingle, partake in, or watch a separate Specialty. It was fun for Brea, and she always enjoyed herself no matter what Specialty her family visited.

There were no buttons for the invisible Healers, or the last four occupied houses in The Neighborhood. Nobody saw the people who belonged to those two other parts of their Neighborhood, and they were a nagging source of Brea's interest. Their grocery stores were run by the people in The Dining part. It was the only part of The Neighborhood they saw on a regular basis, and she had questions about them that were never answered, as well. She pushed the third-floor button, and when the elevator opened she saw the flurry of assistant coaches, students, and Head Coach Fernsbee all hurrying around getting ready for today's tryouts. She found her best friend, Lindy, standing at a mirror straightening out her collar. Lindy had brown hair and blue eyes, and Brea could tell she was nervous.

She walked up behind Lindy and said with a smile, "How many times have you fixed that collar of yours?"

"About 100!" replied Lindy in an exasperated voice.

"Oh, for goodness sakes, you're silly! You look great, and you'll see we will both get promoted today," said Brea with confidence.

"That's easy for you to say. You're ranked number one!"

"Come on Lindy, Let's get in line."

She made no comment to her friends' mention of her ranking.

"Where's Dillin?" asked Brea.

"Who cares!?! He'll probably be in a mood, anyway," retorted Lindy.

"Don't be like that. I don't think he can help it," replied Brea.

A change had come over their friend about four years ago. Before then, they were inseparable, but now it was Brea who stayed closer to Dillin. She did not mind the sullen moods he got into at times, but it rubbed Lindy the wrong way. Head Coach Fernsbee blew his whistle, and it was time for the 20 students who were trying out to get in line. Brea pulled Lindy next to her, and then felt an arm poking her on the other side. Sure enough, it was Dillin, and he was smiling down at her with his root beer-colored eyes and wavy black hair. She smiled right back at him.

Coach Fernsbee then walked up and down the line of the 20 students, and made sure they were dressed correctly, shoes shined, and that everything was in order.

"Okay, students. You know the drill," said the Head Coach. "The man will be here in a few minutes, and I will call you two at a time to tryout. Any 18-year-old students that do not get promoted will be seen by me for further instructions after the announcements have been made." Coach Fernsbee ended by saying, "Focus, and Good Fortune to all of you." He said this every year.

When the man walked in the back door, Brea caught her breath. He was impeccably dressed in what was sure to be a designer suit. She knew this by watching her personal screen and learning about all the fashion choices of The Elites. He wore a diamond ring, and a diamond watch. Jewelry was not available in The Neighborhoods, but she admired it and wondered what piece of jewelry she would pick out first when she was promoted. No one knew if he was a representative of The Elites, or one of them. It didn't matter. The man was here, and Brea couldn't wait to tryout, be promoted, and begin her new life.

He shook Coach Fernsbee's hand, gave him a greeting, and then the first two names were called. One student tripped down the 3 stairs to the Gaming floor, and this immediately disqualified her. No mistakes like this were tolerated, and the 16-year-old walked over and sat in one of the 10 chairs students took when not chosen. Another student's name was called out, and it was Lindy. Both students did very well and took their place back in line. Brea wanted to squeeze her friend's hand to congratulate her but knew this would not be allowed. It was not professional. When Brea's name was called along with an accomplished 18-year-old, she excelled past all expectations. Brea was fast, caught a cheater, and ran the end of a Bridge Match to perfection. She took her place back in line and waited. Dillin was among the last two called, and they were both remarkable.

The man had been taking notes the entire time, and quickly handed the piece of paper with the names to Coach Fernsbee and whispered something to him. Coach then called out the names of the students to be promoted. Brea, Lindy, and Dillin were not on the list. Not one of them! All three took their places in the remaining chairs left for those not picked and watched the 10 students who left to join The Elites with pride and happiness all over their faces. Brea could not help but feel anger inside but did not show it. To show anger would not be considered professional, but she felt it all the same. Brea lowered her head, and Coach saw this. He walked up to her and offered some advice.

"I know you're disappointed, but things happen for a reason. Even if we don't understand them at the time," said Coach Fernsbee.

This did not comfort her in any way, at all.

"Number One, Coach. I'm ranked number one, and Lindy and Dillin are ranked in the top 10 along with me. All three of us are Gaming Masters, but the man took EVERY 18-year-old! How did this happen?" and on that question, Brea ended her controlled rant.

"Brea," Coach said a little firmer, "Don't question how or why too much. It will only lead to bad ends, and it will not help you with your attitude ranking."

There were many things connected to rankings besides skill, and attitude was one of them. She knew this and knew better, but this was taxing the limits on her patience, and sense of fairness. Coach stood back and told the 10 remaining students that since none of them left were 18, they all had next season to look forward to, and hoped to see some of them tonight at The Social. That was it. All her hard work, her ranking, and her talent had received nothing in return. She felt like she had been kicked in the stomach.

Brea stood up, and turned to walk out, but Lindy caught her by the hand.

"I'm so sorry. I was certain YOU would get promoted."

"Thanks, but I thought all three of us would be picked, and we should have been," replied Brea to her friend, and asked, "Hey, where did Dillin go off to now?"

"Are you kidding?" questioned Lindy, and added, "He's probably off sulking somewhere, and there's no telling about what."

"Stop being so hard on him," said Brea and asked, "What is your problem?"

"Look, I still care about DIllin, but I wish he would just get over himself and whatever he's going through," said an exasperated Lindy.

"Maybe I'll find out," she replied.

"Brea, you've tried and got nothing out of him. He's like one of those clams on the beaches we see on our screens. Slammed shut!"

"Before I go find him, I have to face my family," she replied with sadness in her voice.

"Bye. I'll see you tonight," said Lindy as they went home to their families.

When Brea got off the elevator at her home on the first floor, her mom was standing there. Obviously, her mom had heard the elevator and grabbed on to her and held her tight.

"I know you are sorry about the outcome of your tryout," said her mom quietly, "But I'm so glad to have you home with us."

This somewhat bewildered Brea. She didn't think of her and her mom being all that close, but maybe her mom was keeping her feelings bottled up from having her husband taken away. When she looked in her Mother's eyes, she knew it was true. Her face was flooded with relief. Brea knew for the first time that her mom didn't want to lose her, and it made her feel very conflicted. She was happy to know her mom truly cared about her, but didn't she want her daughter to be an Elite? It was an honor. A privilege. What a confusing day this was turning out to be!

At least Brea knew what was waiting for her on the third floor. As soon as she entered her grandma's room, she didn't even have her Headgear on. She was standing, and had her arms stretched out to her. Brea ran into them and sobbed. She could always be herself with her, and the pain of the rejection just flowed out.

Her Grandma just held her tight, and said, "I know, sweet thing."

She kept repeating this phrase to Brea until she stopped crying. Her Grandma sat back in her chair, and Brea knelt at her feet putting her head in her lap.

"I just don't know how I can do better than being ranked number one," and asked, "What more can I accomplish to be promoted?"

Her Grandma sighed and said, "I don't know dear heart, but I'm happy to have you for one more season. Guess I'm selfish, wanting to keep you with me, and don't want to lose any more of my family to The Elites."

This raised Brea's head, and she looked at her with surprise. This was the first time she had ever spoken with regret about her son being taken away.

"Grandma, you know at least half of us end up getting promoted," said Brea and avoided the uncomfortable subject of her dad.

"I know," she replied, "But you could always end up an assistant coach or get married, and then I wouldn't lose you at all."

Brea was in disbelief! Her Grandma knew how much being promoted to be an Elite meant to her.

"Does this have anything to do with my Father?" she asked. She had to know after this revelation.

"Partly," said her Grandma, "It's true my son should have never left this family, but I accepted and made peace with that long ago. Those were different times, and they needed doctors. Your Father had been overlooked in some confusion that was going on at the time."

"Confusion of what kind?"

"You don't need to know any of that, my sweet girl."

"Oh brother! Here we go again! I can't ask about anything," she replied with obvious frustration.

"That's not true," said her Grandma.

"Okay, tell me what goes on in the last four houses on this block?" asked the 17-year-old.

"How many times do I have to tell you that I don't know? And did you ever stop to think it's a good thing?"

"No. I think we should know everything about our Neighborhood, and it's only natural to be interested," stated Brea in a superior tone.

Her Grandma laughed out loud and said, "Interested are we? You've always been this way but sometimes, as the old saying goes, ignorance is bliss."

Brea looked at her and rolled her eyes with a smile.

"Okay Grandma. You win this round, but I'm never going to think ignorance is bliss," then she added, "I'm gonna look for Dillin."

She kissed her goodbye and went outside to see if Dillin was in the trees across from their houses. There he was sitting next to one, and had a dark look on his face. This was not going to stop her. Brea was determined to push past his mood, and not be put off this time. Today she was going to find out what was wrong with her friend.

Chapter Three

"What's up?" asked Brea.

"Nothing. I'm just thinking," replied Dillin.

"I'm really disappointed about none of us getting promoted," said Brea.

"Is that all you care about? Don't you care about anything else?" asked Dillin.

"Are you kidding me, or what? You know I care about you, Lindy, and my family!" Brea said upset at her brooding friend.

"Forget it," replied Dillin with a resigned voice that finally got Brea agitated enough to blow up in his face.

"Dillin, what in the heck is wrong with you? What happened to my friend?" asked Brea and went on. "We used to be a lot closer. We used to tell each other everything, but now I can barely get a sentence out of you, and I've just about had it!"

Dillin looked at Brea knowing she was the best friend he would or could ever have. He also knew that to tell his secret could put himself, his grandfather, and her in danger. But Brea loved knowing stuff. Anything. Everything. He also knew he could trust her, and Dillin decided to confide in her if she met his conditions.

"If I tell, you have to promise not to say a word," said Dillin quickly adding, "And I mean it. Especially Lindy. Nobody. Do you get it?"

Dillin's face and voice were full of intensity, and she was convinced that he meant every word.

"I promise you. I won't say anything," replied Brea with earnest sincerity.

Dillin led Brea up to the third floor of his house and opened the door to his grandfather's room. Dillin put up his index finger to his mouth to signify "no talking" and led Brea into the room. Dillin's Grandfather saw them both, and his eyes widened. Dillin went over to him, and they exchanged a few short notes back and forth. The Grandfather just shrugged his shoulders, and waved Brea over. He then stood up and pulled up a wooden plank on the floor. He reached inside and pulled out an incredibly old book. The contents of this book contained images and words that would alter and change her life forever. Once they left Dillin's house and were back hiding in the trees, they both sat down in the lush green grass.

Brea finally spoke up and said, "I can't believe all the things we saw in that book!" and asked Dillin, "What does it mean?"

He replied: "Well, you saw it. You can read. You can see," and continued on, "That was how this place was before."

Brea inquired, "Before what?"

Dillin replied with a fair amount of exasperation in his voice, "I don't know. Before it was THIS!"

Brea thought for a few minutes and said, "So, almost everyone drove a car like in the pictures?"

Dillin replied, "Yes! Everyone had cars. Did you see the motorcycle?"

She said, "Yeah, but it looked dangerous to me."

Dillin responded, "I bet it's an amazing vehicle to ride on!"

"Do you wanna know what I liked?" asked Brea.

"What?"

She said, "I like the picture of that lady holding that dog. I thought the dog was beautiful."

So, I bet you liked the cats too," replied Dillin.

"I thought the cats were pretty, but I would love to have a dog. I was very drawn to all the dogs I saw," said Brea.

"Well, we can't have any of that stuff here," retorted Dillin

Brea blew past her friend's statement and said, "That thing flying up high in the sky was called an Air a Plane?"

Dillin corrected her, saying, "No, that's close, but it's pronounced Airplane. That's how people used to travel. They used to travel in cars, motorcycles, airplanes, trains, and those tiny boats."

Brea asked, "Travel where, and why don't we have any of those things here? Not even what that little kid was riding on. What was it?"

Dillin answered his friend, "A bicycle."

"Yeah, a bicycle. I'd like one of those, too, but not a train. Everyone appeared to be cramped in those. Why don't we have any of it?"

"I have no idea. All I know is my Grandfather was willing to show me these things a few years ago. He showed me that book because he wanted me to know something. That it used to be different before this, and that there was something outside of The Neighborhood," replied Dillin.

"You mean, you think all those things exist outside The Neighborhood?"

Dillin said, "I don't know, but I think so. I think about it all the time."

It was like a light was turned on in Brea's head! And she said, "No wonder you spend so much time alone thinking and brooding to yourself! I don't know what I'd do with all this information. It would probably drive me crazy!"

Dillin shot her daggers and said, "Hey, Brea…."

But before he could go any further, she cried, "I know! I know! And I'm not gonna say anything to anybody! The only person I'm going to talk about this with is you, okay? I promised, and so I won't say a word."

"Good! So, what else did you like?"

Brea answered, "Well, the people dancing in that beautiful room looked nice. The kids on the slide into that tiny square of water looked like fun."

Dillin replied, "Those tiny squares of water were called: swimming pools, and kids and adults swam in them for fun and exercise."

"Oh. How do you know all this?" asked Brea.

"My grandpa has been telling me through notes about everything he knows."

Brea thought to herself for a few minutes, and tried to take it all in. Then she asked, "Those tiny yachts. What are they called? I forgot."

"They're called boats. Lots of people had boats back then. You didn't have to be an Elite to have one, but mostly people who lived near water had them."

"Dillin, I really liked the boats, and think it would be fun to ride in one." Then Brea asked, "What was that book anyway?"

"I think it's called a travel guide. That's what my Grandpa told me, anyway," replied Dillin, and he continued, "When people went to what my Grandpa calls a job or a vacation, they would use all these things to travel there."

"REALLY!?!"

"Yeah! Say if it were possible to go somewhere else from The Neighborhood, we would use those things to get there. From what my Grandpa says, people used to do that all the time!" explained Dillin.

Brea responded, "Those rooms were so luxurious, and the buildings were so beautiful! I just can't believe people used to live this way, and just maybe somewhere they still do!"

"I don't know about that. According to my Grandpa nobody lives that way anymore, but maybe The Elites do. My grandpa thinks they don't."

"Why? What else did your Grandpa tell you."

"Look, Brea, all I know from him is that something really bad happened a long time ago when my Grandpa was a young man. It was terrible, and so awful that it changed the whole world, and that's all my Grandpa will tell me."

Brea asked her friend, "I wonder what it was?"

Snorting a laugh, Dillin said, "Well, forget about finding out! That's all I've been able to get out of him, and I'm family. Don't think he'll be telling you. He wasn't that happy about me bringing you up there."

"I get it. I was just wondering."

"Okay. Anyway, I've been thinking a lot about traveling myself," said Dillin.

Her eyes gleamed, "For real? To where?"

Brea saw Dillin's eyes looking deeper into the trees, and he said, "You know, these trees seem to go back forever, but I bet they end somewhere. Do you want to go and see where they end?"

"You think they may take us to where the dogs, cars, bicycles, and boats are?"

"Don't ask me, but I think it's worth a shot to find out," answered Dillin.

Brea said in a heartbeat, "Okay, I'll go with you!"

"Alright, let's meet in the early morning. We do have The Social tonight."

"Yeah, but I'm really happy. We get to go to The Dining part of The Neighborhood. It's my favorite."

"The food's great, but all that correct fork, correct spoon, sit up straight, and napkin crap is for the birds!" said Dillin.

"But that's part of our schooling and training. It's etiquette," replied Brea.

"I know, and I still think it's a bunch of crap! Our family is going to the Athletics part of The Neighborhood, and that's fun! I hope they'll be putting on a Football Game tonight."

"If that's what you want to see, I hope you get to," said Brea.

Dillin stood and gave Brea a hand up. The two friends left the privacy of the trees, walked back to their homes, and joined their families to go to: The Social.

Chapter Four

Brea was up early and dressed in her most comfortable jeans and sneakers. She packed a sandwich, an apple, and a couple of bottles of water. She had no way of telling how long it would take them to get to the end of the trees, and she wanted to be prepared. She left her home and found Dillin already waiting for her.

"You can't wait to get started?" asked Brea.

"As nosy as you are, I'm surprised you weren't out here before sunrise!"

Brea gave him a scowl and said, "Let's go."

The two started their trek, and it was fun. They did see different types of trees as they got deeper. These trees were taller and had wider trunks. The branches started higher up the tree, and there were some that were very short and stubby. It made walking more like weaving through big patches of grass. No bush or flowering plant looked like this, and the actual grass was becoming more infrequent. As they walked, they talked about these differences, but Dillin also brought up The Social they had been to the night before.

"It wasn't a Football Game in Athletics. It was Gymnastics," Dillin said while making a face.

Brea laughed and said, "I know you don't like Gymnastics. Sorry."

"You're not sorry or you wouldn't be laughing! At least we didn't go to the Horticulture part of our Neighborhood, that's the worst. Watching how they make the fertilizer. That's gross. Teaching about the bees, butterflies, and hummingbirds is boring. Listening to them talk about how they are in charge of keeping our Neighborhood beautiful is only bragging rights. The tools they show us to demonstrate how they trim, prune, and cut everything are alright, but that's it."

"Stop being a baby. It's not the end of the world, ya know!" replied Brea, and continued on. "We had a fabulous dinner of some kind of shellfish with melted butter, creamed noodles, broccoli, a gorgeous salad, soft rolls, and I had chocolate cake for dessert."

"I know what you had for dessert. You always have chocolate cake. Don't you ever want to try anything else?"

"No. Nothing in the grocery store can compare to the chocolate cake in the Dining part of The Neighborhood. It's so light, soft, and creamy."

"Oh brother," sighed Dillin.

"Oh, be quiet," said Brea with sarcasm.

"Dillin, why do you think your Grandfather told you about the old days?"

"He was told that if he talked about any of this to his children they would all be dead, but they didn't say anything about their grandchildren," replied Brea's friend.

"So, we could get in trouble for knowing these things. Couldn't we?"

"Yeah. That's why it's so important not to tell anyone."

They continued their walk in silence, and regardless of the shade provided by the trees it started getting hot. They had been walking for hours. Brea regretted not grabbing a hat. Dillin had one on, and she felt like taking it from him. She reached her hand out to swat it, but Dillin saw her out of the corner of his eye and ran away as they both laughed. Brea couldn't keep up with him, and he was way in front of her.

"Hey! I need some water," called out Brea and added, "Slow down."

"That's what you get for trying to steal my hat!" yelled Dillin as he turned to continue.

"Are you gonna wait for me?" asked Brea.

"You can see me just fine. Drink your water and come on. We don't have all day!" replied Dillin over his shoulder as he kept walking, but he did slow down.

Brea drank the water, and then poured some over her head to cool down. This felt great, and she got to her feet to catch up with him. As she was getting closer to her friend, she saw Dillin fall to the ground! She ran to him as fast as she could. Did he hit a tree? A low hanging branch? Dillin was tall and strong, but something had him lying flat on his back, holding his nose, and yelling.

"Damn it! Damn it!" was all Dillin kept yelling as Brea reached and bent over him.

"What happened?" asked a concerned Brea.

"I don't know, but my nose hurts like heck!"

"Let me see," replied Brea.

Dillin took his hands off his nose, and it was already starting to swell. What was going on? She looked around but didn't see any big branches hanging low. In fact, the thickness of the trees had been thinning but not the bushes. She stepped forward with an instinctive hand in front of her, and suddenly Brea felt something stop her in her tracks. She felt it. She hit it. She walked along the length, and it seemed to not end. She could see trees on their side, and tall trees on the other, but this clear barrier was separating both sides from each other.

Dillin yelled out to her, "Why are you still looking at stuff? Get back over here and help me!"

Brea ran back to her friend and said, "You ran into an invisible barrier of some kind."

"Are you kidding me? Have you lost your mind?" questioned Dillin as he held a rag drenched in water to his nose.

Brea said softly, "Is there anything I can do? You're not bleeding, are you?"

Blood was rarely seen in The Neighborhood. It scared everyone, and it was a sign to push the button for the invisible Healers. If Dillin was bleeding, she would have to run home regardless of the circumstances and get him help.

"No. I'm not bleeding, but it hurts," replied Dillin.

"Are you injured to the point you can't get up?" she asked.

"I guess I can get up."

Brea's tone changed, she put her hands on her hips and said, "I have NOT lost my mind! There's something ahead that stops us from going any further, and if you had been running it probably would have broken your nose or worse!"

Dillin looked up at her with dismay and said, "I still hurt."

"If you're not bleeding and can get up, we need to check this thing out!" said a frantic Brea.

"Okay. Okay, I'm getting up."

They walked towards what they could not see with their hands outstretched. When they touched the invisible barrier, they both looked at each other in disbelief. They could see the same thing. Trees on their side, and trees on the other, but they could not walk towards them any further.

"Let's keep walking along, and see if there is an opening," said Dillin.

"I don't think whoever built this had walking through it in mind," replied Brea.

"Just keep walking. What a know it all you are," said her friend in a teasing voice.

They continued along the barrier keeping their hands on it. When they were about a half of a mile down, there was a clearing. It was an extremely small one, but it was there. The trees were sparse, and they stared into baren brown earth. This was totally alien to Brea and Dillin, and It was ugly. Not only a few trees, but no flowers or bushes. All of a sudden, they heard a combination of muffled sounds. For a couple of seconds, they both saw a flying metal contraption about seven feet in the air chasing people that were running for their lives, and they were covered in black and brown mud! Once Brea and Dillin were over their shock and surprise, they turned back for home without a word. Dillin's nose was quite swollen, and it needed to be iced. They had to get home as fast as they could.

Brea finally said, "Those people just didn't look like they'd been caked in mud, but they looked scared."

"Wouldn't you be with that flying contraption chasing after you?" Dillin stated as both a fact and a question.

"Of course, I would."

Dillin thought for a few seconds and asked, "I wonder what that flying thing is?"

"That's your big concern? What about the people? They were terrified!" exclaimed Brea.

Dillin's thoughts were on a different plane altogether, and he said, "Hey, do you think if they have something like that on the other side, they might have cars, too?"

"I don't know, but who cares?"

Their conversation remained this way. Dillin was preoccupied with the flying vehicle, and the prospect of cars. Brea was focused more on the condition of the people. When they were finally across from their houses, Dillin stopped Brea with his arm and said he had something to ask her. When they were seated in the grass, he attempted to begin, but Brea spoke up first.

"Were we dreaming?"

"The same thing? That's completely impossible," replied Dillin.

"We both want to find out, though. Don't we?" Brea questioned her friend.

"I'm counting on that because you want to know everything," said Dillin in a knowing voice.

"I only ask about things that I believe we have the right to get answers to," she said defensively.

Brea received a knowing look by Dillin, and he said, "Of course. Jeez Brea, who do you think you're talking to?"

"Well, I can't help that I was born inquisitive by nature."

"That's the understatement of the year! But it's okay with me," replied Dillin and asked, "Do you wanna go find out what's on the other side or not?"

"How? The barrier is in the way."

"We could walk to the end of The Neighborhood and see if there's a way to get over there," the young man explained.

"No one ever walks past their own part of The Neighborhood," said Brea.

"But we could give it a try. If we stay hidden in the trees, but not far enough to lose sight of the sidewalk, no one will see to turn us back," replied Dillin.

Brea was impressed with his plan and said, "That's a fantastic idea, and I think it may work. Hey, what if we do find a way over? We might be gone longer than a day. We have to think about this."

Dillin said, "No. We have our week off after Promotion Day. This is the perfect chance to go find out. We can at least try."

Brea answered, "If we just disappear, our families will worry about us. And you know what happens if we don't sit in our chairs at least every 72 hours."

Every youngster's chair was linked up to The Healers, and if a child didn't sit in their chair for 3 days running, it set off an alarm. They were all taught this, and each kid did as they were told. In fact, the kids loved looking at their personal screens. It was meant to be mainly educational, but the children found their screens to be extremely entertaining, as well.

"You need to ice your nose, and we need to come up with a plan for our families," said Brea.

"Okay. I'll meet you in front of your house in an hour, we can go for a walk, and figure this out," said Dillin.

"What are you going to tell your parents about your nose?"

"That I fell out of a tree," answered Dillin, and laughed because he never fell out of trees.

"Think they'll believe it?" asked Brea, and after he nodded she said, "I'll be outside my house after sunset."

"You and your sunsets! You still watch them every single evening? asked Dillin.

"Of Course! That's the stupidest thing to ask ME!" exclaimed Brea. "Whatever. See ya later."

Chapter Five

When Brea entered her home, her mind was spinning! She couldn't wrap her head around everything that had transpired. More than anything, she could not forget the look of terror in the eyes of those poor people covered in mud. Brea had to calm down and began to think of what she would be doing if this was a regular day. But it wasn't a regular day. Not in the least. She thought, and she thought some more. What had she done last year after not getting promoted? She remembered and went to her chair. She sat down and pushed the button. Up popped her personal screen, and she pressed a number to observe her performance as she did last year. This didn't help a bit. She watched her tryout, and it was flawless. Brea could not find a single mistake, hesitation, or presentation error. Watching this was only getting her angry all over again, and nothing would be gained by that.

It was time to go upstairs to the third floor. It was something Brea did every day in the early evening. Brea knocked on her Grandma's door, and went in. They squeezed each other's hand, and Brea walked out to the balcony. The sunset was beginning. Already, the oranges, reds, yellows, and pinks in the sky were magnificent. This was not what she was waiting for, though. As the sun went below the mountains and trees on the horizon, it happened. The straight and perfect line of purple that seemed to come out of the sun itself shot into the air, and then fanned out across the evening sky! It was the most beautiful thing she ever beheld.

It lasted quite a while. When it grew darker, it was breathtaking! A purple and blackish sky with stars dotted along the edges. It was, as far as Brea was concerned, perfection. There were times the purple was far away in the distance. At other times, it was so close it appeared to be happening at the end of her Neighborhood. Her Grandma told her it had something to do with the earth's rotation around the sun. It made no difference to her. Brea had been fascinated and captivated by her sunsets since she was a child, and not a single thing kept her from viewing them.

She left her Grandma's room and went to take a walk with Dillin to discuss their plans for tomorrow. Brea had an idea of her own and wanted to tell him. He was not going to like it. When she stepped outside, Dillin was waiting for her, and she got on with it.

"Dillin, we have to tell Lindy before we go."

"I told you, no. NO Lindy!"

"We have to Dillin. What if we find a way over there, and are gone longer than a day? We need a cover story. I'm not going to tell her the truth. Really, I'm not. I will say that we are going back into the trees to see if we can find different kinds of them. Different flowers and bushes. If we are gone longer than a day, they will only be looking for us in the trees in front of our homes, and they won't bother any other Specialty."

Dillin thought about this and said, "Maybe you're right, but Lindy has been a jerk to me for a long time. I'm not sure if it's her I want to tell."

"And you? You haven't been a jerk yourself for years, and who else is there to tell? I'll give her notes to give to our parents. As long as we are home before 72 hours goes by, we'll be fine," explained Brea.

"And if we are not home in 72 hours?" asked Dillin.

"We both already know. The alarms will go off in every Specialty in the Neighborhood, and that's that."

"In that case, we gotta make sure we get back in time," said Dillin.

"No kidding, you brainless thing," said Brea and added, "Write your note. I'll pick it up in a few minutes."

"Whose idea and plan to go was this, anyway?" asked Dillin.

"Yours. I just made it a better one," answered a smiling Brea.

After this exchange, Dillin didn't know if he wanted her to go with him or thrash the life out of her instead. She could be such a pain, but he went home and wrote the note. Once Brea picked it up and had both notes in sealed envelopes, she went to Lindy's house and asked if they could walk together for a little while. She told Lindy her and Dillin's plan to search back into the trees.

"Have you two gone and lost your marbles?" asked Lindy.

"No, and with our break from training it's the best time to go," replied Brea.

"Well, I think this plan is ridiculous, and for no good reason. What could you hope to accomplish?"

"We might be able to add information about other types of trees and flowers we know nothing about. Plus, I think it will do Dillin a lot of good. Haven't seen him this excited or interested about anything in a long time," explained Brea.

"You're putting me in a bad situation. They will blame me," said Lindy.

"No, they won't. The notes are sealed, and you are to give them to my mom and Dillin's parents in the afternoon. What would they blame you for?" asked Brea.

"I don't know. I don't like this," said Lindy.

"We want to do it, and you're the only one we can trust. Our parents would never give permission. There's no other way to do this except to take off and go."

"You two are taking a big chance. You can't know what's really back there. What if there's trouble? What if you get hurt?" replied and asked Lindy.

"Why do you think we are leaving these notes for our families? If we are not home by nightfall, our parents and friends can look for us. I don't think there will be any trouble, and we will probably be home before dark," said Brea as she tried to console and convince Lindy.

"Okay. I'll do it, but I'm only doing it for you. Dillin is just proving he's becoming more of a nut case with this idiotic idea!" said Lindy.

"Thank you so much," said Brea as she hugged her friend in relief.

"I have to get back home, and you need a good nights' sleep," replied Lindy.

"Don't worry," said Brea.

"You know I'll be worried until you get back. You're my best friend."

"And you're mine."

They walked back to Lindy's house, and Brea gave Lindy the two envelopes. Both were simply marked. One had the word mom on the front, and the other had the words, mom and dad. That was easy enough to distinguish one from the other. The two girls hugged each other good night, and Brea went home. When she got up to her room, she pulled out her gaming backpack. She put in an extra pair of jeans with a jacket to match, another blouse, sweater, underwear, and socks in case they were delayed for a night. The rest of it, like food and water, could wait until morning. She tossed and turned all night. Sleep was elusive to Brea, and she would drift off only to quickly awaken. The thought of tomorrow's adventure was too nerve wracking and exciting at the same time for sleep. Brea was certain she got less than two hours of sleep the entire night.

Before the crack of dawn, Brea and Dillin were on their way. They both prepared for being gone longer than a day. They had packs with a change of clothes, food, water, and were wearing jackets. Brea's jacket was the color of green and black, and Dillin's was a solid dark green. They wanted to blend into the trees the best they could. They spoke in whispers, kept far enough in the trees, but didn't lose sight of the sidewalk. Their Neighborhood was longer than they thought, and about halfway there they noticed that the mountain range and trees were an optical illusion of some kind. This was a multi-layered rock wall!

The colors were varied in different browns, greens, yellows, and even some blue, but this was nothing but rocks. They were huge, jagged, and stacked rocks. When they finally reached the end, they cranked their heads as far back as they could, but still could not see the top. Why didn't anyone tell them about the rock wall, thought Brea? She remembered that she had assumed but had never asked anyone. They left the trees and walked between the wall and The Dining part of their Neighborhood. As they got into position to observe the goings on, Brea and Dillin were in for quite a few sights that left them stupefied.

It was almost dark, but there were large lights that lit up the end of The Dining part of the Neighborhood. Trucks were coming and going. Trucks that weren't supposed to exist anymore. Boats were coming into shore and were also under the category of nonexistent. Dillin told Brea that this had to be a lake because there were no waves crashing onto the sand. People were cutting up fish and wrapping them in paper. These fish were put into boxes and loaded onto the trucks and driven away behind the rock wall. Other trucks arrived bringing boxes to The Dining Part, and they were all marked by Specialty. As she watched in amazement, Brea's mind was whirling with questions.

Why was the rock wall layered? Why didn't they know about the lake, the boats, the trucks, and the fish? What the heck was going on around here? They observed the strange interactions as the trucks would drive in and thought it odd that no words were spoken. It was only packing, marking, loading, and unloading. Neither Brea nor Dillin recognized anyone from The Dining Part of the Neighborhood. There was a door, and it looked like some kind of weird elevator. They put the boxes inside, pushed a button, and the boxes were lowered. Brea couldn't help herself, and finally spoke.

"Do you have any idea what's going on here?" asked Brea.

"No, and I don't understand why it's happening without our knowledge," replied Dillin.

It was about then that he saw a boat coming to shore in the dead of night. It had a beam of light that encompassed the full front of it, and it pulled right onto land. The man exited the boat without any fish, or anything else. His Grandfather had shown him a drawing of a boat like this one. It had just two buttons. One had a picture of the sun that started it up and shut it off, and the other button had a stream of white light that lit up the front of the boat. Dillin knew this was the vehicle that they would take to continue their adventure. It would be easy, right? Wrong. Brea had strong objections. As a matter of fact, she was flabbergasted at the suggestion for once in her life.

"This is ridiculous! We've seen things that we know nothing about. Things concerning The Neighborhood that we have no answers for, but you want to take a boat and, get us caught, hurt, or killed?"

"I can't believe it! You're the most curious person in the world but want to stop now? You want to find out about the people on the other side that are covered in mud, and I want to find out about cars. We saw trucks drive in and drive outta here and go wherever. Brea, every truck is gone, but the boat is right there. We'll use it to get to the other side," said Dillin.

"Those huge lights are off, and I can barely see a thing," replied Brea.

Dillin stuck out one of his fingers and said, "There are lanterns lit around here. Look where I'm pointing. You can make out the boat, and I know how to drive it."

"Lindy's right! You are a nut case! You've never been in a boat in your life, and suddenly you're an expert! If you could get it going, where would we go?" asked an angry Brea.

Dillin answered, "The Neighborhood ends or begins here, and if we take the boat along the rock wall, it will end too. It seems logical to me. When that happens, we will make a left, and hopefully make it to the other side."

"Do you honestly believe that?" Brea questioned her buddy.

"I do. I believe this is our best opportunity to find out, and finally figure out what the flying flock is going on around here. There are plenty of mysteries about what we've seen here tonight, but we can't find out. I didn't recognize one person from The Dining part of The Neighborhood. Did You?"

Brea shook her head and said, "No."

"We don't know anything, but we could start learning by taking off in that boat," said Dillin.

And that's exactly what they did. The pair crept along the edge of the wall, and down to the sand. Once they reached the boat, they tossed in their packs, pushed the boat into the lake, got in, and took off. Dillin pushed the button with the sun on it and turned it around to face the vastness of the lake. The button to light up the front was next, and it gave them excellent sight. They could see well in front of themselves and began their journey along the massive rock wall.

Brea was awestruck. It was a gorgeous night, and on the lake it was peaceful and quiet. No noise whatsoever. Brea was so used to the birds chirping in her part of The Neighborhood, she didn't realize the difference. This silence was tranquil. The gentle motion of the boat was both calming and soothing. The breeze in her hair from the air flow gave her tingles down her spine. For his part, Dillin stayed close to the rock wall. He didn't deviate away from it but thought better of hugging the wall because there might be rocks under the water he could not see. After some time had passed, Dillin could see the end of the wall.

"Do you see? Do you see the end of the wall, Brea?"

"Dillin, I see it!" replied the excited girl.

Along with the end of the wall came the sound of rushing water. Neither of them knew what to make of it and looked at each other quizzically.

"What is that?"

"Don't ask me," replied Dillin.

The sound of this rushing water began to get louder, and closer. It was also starting to pull the boat towards it.

Brea was anxious and said, "Make this boat go faster and turn it away from the rushing sound. Get us away from it!"

"I don't know how to make the boat go faster, and turning it to the right isn't working," replied Dillin.

They could both feel the boat being pulled towards this rushing sound.

"Turn the boat away! Turn it away! NOW!" screamed Brea.

"I can't! Something is pulling the boat to it. There's nothing I can do!" screamed back a frustrated Dillin.

The boat turned left on its own, and there was nothing in front of them but an abyss of blackness. The light gave the two explorers their next glimpse of what was coming. It was white water falling without anything else in sight.

"Oh No! Oh NO!" yelled both Brea and Dillin.

As the boat flew down the raging white water, they both hung on for dear life screaming at the top of their lungs!

PART TWO

THE NEW WORLD ORDER

Chapter Six

About 55 years ago, a Global Pandemic had struck the human race for a second time. Millions were infected and died, but its effect on the men and women in politics was strange. Of course, those in Government had the quickest testing and received the medications to help them long before the masses, but they seemed indifferent to the suffering of the general population. It seemed slower than the first time around. The acknowledgement was quicker, but the aggressiveness to deal with the Pandemic was not. The leaders in Banking, Technology, and large Corporations were having peculiar revelations of their own. They were noticing that even though unemployment was more widespread, it was still not affecting them. In fact, it was improving their gains further, and thus began the seeds and alliances of The New World Order.

There was a top secret meeting that included Presidents and Leaders of several key Countries. It was hosted by major CEOs of Top World Banks, the largest Corporations, and Worldwide Tech Companies. In that meeting, they were frank and found they had much in common. Collectively, they were sick and tired of the moaning and groaning from people railing about not getting a fair shake in life, and income inequality. Additionally, there was no appetite for bailing out whom they considered the undeserving and unemployed like they had the first time around. So, their number one goal was to have an entire professional servant society called: A Grove. Each Grove would be sliced into five Territories.

The Territory of The Neighborhoods where their personal servants were to be born and raised. The territory of The Containers where undesirables of their Countries were to be "contained" by others who reveled in the prospect of that kind of power, and these people were given much more freedoms for their services. The Territory of the Growers and Farmers, and they were to be the only Territory that organized religion was allowed. The Territory of The Drivers and Manufacturers who would be local to all parts of a Grove, and they were given vehicles and the ability to travel. Finally, there were The Medical and Science Professionals who were treated with the most respect and had the most freedom than any of the other groups. Only two Territories knew the whole truth about their Grove: The men and women of the Medical and Scientific Territory, and The Territory of the Containers. These men and women who took over the world called themselves: The Elites.

Next came the unleashing of a stronger strain of a Viral Pandemic in certain parts of the world, and it killed almost two billion people in less than a year. The Elites felt that to have their Utopia certain Countries in Central America, Asia, and The Middle East had to be eliminated. The only reason Countries like Russia and Saudi Arabia survived was their willingness to get rid of top-level government personnel threats to total world peace. When those other targeted countries were weakened, The Elites sent in supposed "Diplomatic" groups that were really Militia. Within 2 months, all countries deemed a threat to world peace were under the control and governed by The Elites.

How did these people who took over the world deal with over two billion dead bodies? That was a feat in and of itself. They could not use cremation and add to the air pollution problem and didn't have the manpower or time to bury this many people. What they did have access to were gigantic vats that they converted to boiling and bone meal machines. They didn't want the flesh of diseased bodies, and therefore they were boiled until the flesh was gone, and only the bones remained. Those remains were transferred mechanically to another area to be pulverized into bone meal and used as fertilizers for forests and farms. This decision was made by The Elites in a matter of fact way and is further testament to the brutal commitment they had to the creation of their New World Order.

Number three was dealing with Climate Change. In the privacy of their meetings, no debates existed, and all acknowledged this was a major problem. There were legitimate concerns of other Global Pandemics from permafrost, wet markets, and mutations. In short, Climate Change had to be reversed if they were going to rule and live in all their glory. This gave way to The Global Clean-up. It was a huge success, and many people saw it as real progress in Green Jobs, prosperity, and the saving of our planet. For over 10 years, people from around the world had joined together to the reforestation of the land, and cleaned up the oceans, lakes, rivers, and air.

All vehicles went electric, and there was a device that was built to remove trash, plastic, glass, and metal from the oceans of the world. They had to do something with this discarded and useless debris, and a massive space station was built to store all of it. Over this ten-year period, the earth rebounded dramatically. The ecosystems came alive, the ice caps started to reform, the world temperature dropped by over two degrees, and animal species on the brink of extinction came off the endangered lists by the hundreds. If you did not live-in certain parts of the world and were not over the age of 60, it was a lovely time to be alive.

The fourth and final decision made by The Elites was to eliminate the problem of overpopulation. Anyone over the age of 60 who were not filthy rich, or an expert in a medical or scientific field were viewed as expendable. This proved to be a rather sticking point with some that came to power. There were many arguments about it, but the rationale was that if population control was to be accomplished it must be carried out. They did not want a general senior society that had to be cared for and supported. The Asian Groves were particularly offended because they valued their elders in higher regard than people in the western hemisphere. Their culture, traditions, and morality were affronted to a near breaking point with The New World Order. About two years into their plans, there were reports of better weather, healthier crops, improved air quality, and cleaner water. They could see tangible benefits of the actions they took in real and quick time.

Many other conversations came about from these reports. The convincing argument was that a smaller population would be much more affordable, and easier to control. On that note, their decision was made final. The world was informed of a new variant spreading quickly around the world, and the elder population was the most at risk. The peoples of the globe believed them since it was their group who died in the greatest percentages the first two times around. All the leaders, politicians, CEOS, and many elderly community leaders took the new vaccine in public. This set the general population at ease, and all persons over the age of 60 allowed the administration of this syringe.

Within a few months, many elderly people started to die of seemingly natural causes, and many died in their sleep. What the average person did not know is The Elites were given a placebo, and the senior population were given a special drug that affected them to various degrees according to their own personal overall health. In about a year and a half, over another billion people were dead. Almost without exception, the dead were 60 years or older. These Elites were careful, though. They did give the placebo to many of the undesirables in their parts of the world over the age of sixty. They had other plans for them.

Then came the hammer. They had been perfecting The Container's techniques in The Middle East for over a decade, and each Country was training their own Container Force. Once the dirty work had been done by the general population, The Containers swooped in, and it came time to choose. The Elites were surprised at how many people were willing to become Containers. It was true that they had more freedom and information than most of the Territories in a Grove, but given the task put before them it was still amazing. The Drivers and Manufacturers were easy enough to recruit because they could still deliver goods to all Territories which gave them a suitable amount of mobility and travel. They knew the basic truths about The New World Order, and this was their form of compensation.

The truly faithful either rebelled and were killed, or they chose to be The Growers and Farmers in great numbers. In the minds of The Elites, they decided these people were fools who might feel closer to their God by cultivating the earth and feeding people. It was only in the Territory of The Farmers and Growers that were allowed to build churches and have services. In the opinion of The Elites, religion caused much of the world's problems. Plus, they wanted to be The Gods of this new world, but the world had to be fed and so this was begrudgingly conceded. Each Grove had a Grower and Farmer Territory, and the religion was chosen by the most practiced within that Grove. In most Western Hemisphere Groves, the religion was a form of Christianity.

The Doctors and Nurses had their Hippocratic Oath to heal the sick, and it sucked them into their plans. The scientists were given spacious labs and homes to conduct research to keep an eye open for possible future viruses, and others to tweak and perfect the implementation of total solar power for them, and every Grove they ruled. The Elites also had kept 10 of the biggest telescopes in the world active to keep track of the skies. The most dangerous part of the scientific territory was the special unit created for the deactivation and removal of nuclear warheads around the world. When a warhead was successfully removed, it was placed in a warehouse for the next trip to the space station. These trips took place every three months, and they were separate from the voyages to take regular debris.

The meteorologists were held in the highest regard. They were tasked with keeping track of the world's weather. They supplied The Elites with detailed reports of all manner of progress and changes. Their information was an important part for the use of propaganda. The news that informed the public on the lessening strength and number of hurricanes, tornadoes, floods, and other matters of natural disasters gave The Elites the justification they needed. That their actions were noble, just, correct, and had saved the Earth.

Chapter Seven

The medical doctors and nurses held a different distinction. There were some local to The Territories within a Grove. Some were the private doctors and nurses to The Elites. There were others that were specialists in coming up with drugs to make their presence as little known as possible to The

Neighborhood. Naturally, the private doctors and nurses to The Elites had the most freedom, full knowledge of their new world, and they were treated almost as equals. Almost. They were the only ones who were gifted with jewelry, professionally trained servants, and occasional invitations to entertainment performances. They had no money, but they had everything else they could want. And we cannot forget the plastic surgeons. The vanity of The Elites was boundless, and they were highly valued, as well.

Doctors, nurses, and anesthesiologists in The Neighborhood part of every Grove were kept a mystery. If a child had an accident, class was cancelled for a time, a button was pushed to inform the invisible healers, the child was given a special liquid to drink which put them to sleep and left on a specialty table. A medical assistant picked them up at a side door no one knew anything about and brought them back by the same method. They tried everything possible to keep everyone in The Neighborhood part of a Grove as safe as possible. Every baby born had their appendix, tonsils, and adenoids out at birth, and was another reason why there were no vehicles of any kind allowed. They wanted the least amount of death in The Neighborhood because these children, grandchildren, and every generation afterward were being bred mainly for their own personal and various uses.

The doctors, nurses, and their various assistants were given gorgeous homes, no information was withheld from them, and they did have personal servants who cooked and cleaned for them. These servants were generally older people from The Neighborhoods who had been promoted but were no longer useful to The Elites. They were from the secret part of the Neighborhoods and going to the Medical and Scientific Territories as cooks and maids was seen as phase two of their lives. These doctors and nurses could drive anywhere they wished in their part of the Territory, or outside of it into the wastelands. They rarely did drive into the wastelands because it was not particularly picturesque, but they could drive at enormous speeds without the worry of traffic or accidents. Their cars were invulnerable to accidents. These vehicles were practically tanks, but still capable of great acceleration.

Death was another event that was dealt with differently In the Neighborhood. It was usually a grandparent that died of old age. The entire family would gather, and then take the body down to the specialty floor. The medical assistants would pick up the body quickly, and it was taken to a crematorium. It was the only form of burial allowed in the Territories, and The Elites were looking forward to the day every grandparent in every Neighborhood was dead, and all their secrets with them.

And it was The Neighborhoods that proved to be the biggest problem in the beginning. Even though they were to live extremely comfortable lives with no bills and no worries, they had little freedom. The Neighborhood would be the most uninformed and ignorant Territory of a Grove. No cars, motorcycles, bicycles, travel, pets, or outside news. The Elites wanted them totally focused on learning how to be proper and excellent servants for them.

In the end, it took a device and a promise. They recruited young parents in their mid-twenties to early thirties with children no more than four years old. What they gave these young couples in return was a virtual reality device that they could put on and relive those years saving the planet, and all the wonderful memories that it entailed. They were told they could never tell their children about the old days, and if they did their entire family would be killed. Every virtual reality set was designed for that person only, and no one else could use it.

The promise was that all couples who volunteered could live out their entire lives in The Neighborhood. No mysterious deaths after the age of 60, and that any health problems would be taken care of by The Healers. Of course, they viewed the promise warily. The Elites just took whatever they wanted whenever they wanted it. As time went by, they saw that the promise was kept. The first few elders over 60 years of age had various health problems, but The Elites took them in secret, treated them with new medicines, and brought them back cured or pain free. They were the only territory that was allowed a true elderly population. It was a strong inducement to become a willing part of The Neighborhood Territory within a Grove.

The Elites took the virtual reality device idea a step further and came up with a chip which they inserted into the children and grandchildren of The Neighborhoods. They sat in a specific chair and pushed a button on that chair. Before the child's eyes popped up a personal screen with scenes from their day. Included were fond memories from family, friends, school, and favorite performances from the Music, Art, and Athletics parts of The Neighborhood. They were also shown beautiful air shots of places that they could live if picked on Promotion Day. There were gorgeous shots of Mansions that The Elites lived in, and extremely large floating homes on the seas called: Yachts.

One of the things Brea liked best was that not one of these places were painted the color green. The thing most common to The Neighborhood was that every home was not only three stories above and three stories below, but that every house was green. They had almost lost all green from the earth in the old days, and they would not be repeating that mistake. So, all The Neighborhoods had green houses with different shades of green painted on the outside by Specialty. They had a green sidewalk for their morning or evening strolls, and they were surrounded by the most beautiful trees, flowers, and bushes that grew around their homes and across from their houses. The Neighborhood was the most beautiful part of every Territory. The Elites felt that The Neighborhoods were the most indulged of any section of a Grove.

Chapter Eight

There were true remarkable advances that were made during this time, and it concerned the elimination of diseases. Cancer, Leukemia, and Diabetes were a thing of the past. Cures for HIV and Aids were discovered. The Elites wanted to live as long as possible, and also wanted their servant society kept healthy. A way that the Scientific and Medical Territories kept in the good graces of The Elites was to come up with these cures. They were not given the most freedom, or the gifts of jewels and servants for nothing.

Hypertension, high cholesterol, and high blood pressure were eliminated by a healthy diet in The Groves. Some of The Elites would suffer at times, but that was only because they indulged too much in foods that caused these ailments. Big Pharma was no longer an option because they all worked for The Elites. If they wanted to keep their elevated status, keeping everyone in excellent health was their only option. They were not able to cure everything. Birth defects would occur on rare occasions. When that happened, the child was euthanized, and it was called a mercy for both the baby and the parents. Maybe these Elites were able to convince themselves of that, but it was simply a way to have the couple move on to having another healthy child to serve them.

Because of the clean air, water, and land the food was healthier. The Territory of The Growers and Farmers no longer used pesticides to grow crops. All fast food restaurants were eliminated, and there was no such thing as processed food. The Elites knew these foods were harmful to people, but they were allowed to flourish in the old days. It was another way of keeping the undesirables of their Countries sick, and it made Big Pharma a ton of money. These foods took years off their life spans, and that was fine by them. However, these practices were stopped, and everyone took their vaccinations and ate healthy.

Certainly, desserts like ice cream, candy, and cakes still existed, but they were made by natural ingredients. No preservatives of any kind were allowed except via canning or by salt. All the children were taught how to cook in The Groves. This just didn't go on in The Dining Specialty. A percentage of the children in every Grove were going to be parents, and they needed to learn how to cook for their families. It was part of everyone's training and continued until they were eighteen. A lot of the food was put together in the Grower and Farmer Territories, and then sent to each of the Grove's Grocery stores. There was no margarine. You asked for butter, and milk was used to make the cakes and ice cream. The milk adults drank was made from almonds. The meat, poultry, and fish were fresh and to be cooked by baking or broiling. Cooking by other methods disappeared, and these choices were made by The Elites to sustain the health of their servant population. Everyone, that is, they chose to be worthy of survival in their New World Order.

The brutality of The Elites came swift and efficiently. If you were considered undesirable and were fortunate enough to see the handwriting on the wall, you and your family fled for your lives. Once that hammer came down and people began having their bank accounts emptied for no other reason than they were not suited for this new world order, they were in confusion and indecisive. Their property and businesses were ransacked, and it didn't matter if you had a few million dollars of worth. That was not enough to be an Elite, and this finally made young and old alike take off for the hills to hide and try to survive.

As a matter of fact, these confiscated monies were used to build the Groves, and their property and businesses were demolished or used to create the different parts of The Territories whenever and wherever it was convenient. The Elites were cut and dry in making these decisions. Their determination to create this New World Order was of paramount importance. Nothing else mattered or got in their way. This was a coordinated worldwide attack of people and hack of wealth. If you were marked as an undesirable of a Country, it did not matter how much wealth that person acquired. One day, a person was worth tens of millions of dollars and property, and the next day that same person was wiped out and worthless.

After a few years of watching billions die, the populous left in the world did as their Countries bid them. On that fateful day, everything was taken off the grid. The Internet was useless, Smartphones were shut off, Landlines cut off, and all that was heard by Radio Communications was nothing but static. The only thing available were the televisions putting out a message by their Emergency Broadcasting Systems. It was the same all over the world, and the message was as follows: Stay in your homes and shelter in place. Please, stay calm and your local Police or Military will be there soon to come to your aid. The vast majority obeyed. Some did not, and it was at their own peril.

Sentiment was of no value. If you were depending on a friendship with an Elite to save you, it was in vain. Many tried to reason with them by stating their prior worth by either education or wealth but going before them was quickly surmised a mistake. These poor unfortunates were briskly taken away, and many of those who were wise enough to flee did not escape. Everyone marked was taken away with their fate's unknown to but a few.

There are many other things about The Elites that could be exposed, revealed, and told. Since the dawn of time, man's inhumanity to man has been a constant of our existence. To further dwell upon them would be a waste. They used the many looming threats of the period as an advantage and gained for themselves total justification for their actions. The land, water, air, and mammals were saved. They reversed Climate Change. They got rid of overpopulation. They had succeeded, and everyone owed them a great debt of gratitude. That's how they saw it and made sure that everyone "in the know" viewed it in the same way.

On the last day of in person meetings, a Tech CEO, who shall remain nameless, said these following remarks at the end of his speech:

"In conclusion, we've used our political puppets to inflame citizens against fellow citizens in several key Countries, and further expanded our own agenda. In destroying the faith of people believing in their elected Governments, we have taken control. A large percentage of the world population is obsessed with using technology in the pursuit of mindlessly playing games, or aspirations of becoming pseudo celebrities. They have been thoroughly distracted. The biggest part of the world's population is busy trying to stay alive or working to make ends meet, and therefore too exhausted to pay attention. That left a minuscule percentile with the ability to care or investigate, and less than nobody listened. On the whole, what we have accomplished here together has been relatively easy. Congratulations to us all."

There is nothing left to be said here about The New World Order, or The Elites. Except this: Brea, Dillin, and Lindy were born in a Neighborhood

Territory. It was part of a place called Summer Grove and located in The Western Hemisphere. This Grove is one among many that used to be called: The United States of America.

PART THREE

THE JOURNEY

Chapter Nine

The lights surrounding the front of the boat never failed and added to the frightening flight down the white water. It was an encompassing mixture of sights and sounds. The crashing against rocks that they could and could not see. There was the raging water roaring in their ears as it spilt over them and into the boat. Screaming words for help where there was none to be had, and the pounding of their hearts that they were sure were going to explode from this unnerving trip that had them both suffering from acute anxiety and the fear of imminent death. Miraculously, the boat finally landed on flat water. They had survived, and spent some minutes catching their breath. Dillin was the first to speak in tones that weren't screams or utter nonsense.

"Are you alright?" Dillin asked Brea.

"I think so, but my leg hurts. I smacked it good against something in here."

"Yeah, I hit my head on the wheel," replied Dillin.

The boat was hit on the side by a wave, and it poured salt water over them and into the boat. Dillin knew immediately that they were no longer in the lake, but an ocean. He turned the boat towards what had to be the shore. Waves did not happen unless you were close to a shoreline and knew this by watching his personal screen. Brea also knew he was doing the right thing but wondered what would happen to them. They were not in The Neighborhood anymore. The waves continued to push them closer to somewhere, but it was still night. They hadn't a clue what was ahead of them.

"Where in the world is this place?" asked Brea.

"I don't know, but we will let these waves take us to shore and find out," replied Dillin.

Since they still had functioning lights. They could see, but only ocean water was before them. Another big wave caught the boat and hurled the two explorers further than any other had, and they found themselves able to see the shoreline. Dillin shut off the boat, and they floated toward the beach. He didn't know how close to shallow water they were and didn't want to chance wrecking the boat after it had survived the white water. He jumped into the sea to find out if he could touch the bottom. He couldn't, but he was close. He lowered himself under the water and found his feet on the seabed. Dillin came back up and told Brea they were almost there. Wherever that was, they hadn't a clue.

"If the boat is turned off, how will we get to land?" asked Brea.

Right on cue, another wave hit the boat, Dillin disappeared under water, and the boat kept floating towards the beach.

"That's how," replied Dillin as he came up gasping for air and climbing back into the boat.

As they got closer, they could see a few vehicles. A couple of them they both recognized, but some they weren't able to distinguish. One of them was a bright red car. Dillin was overcome with excitement. He got out of the boat, and grabbed the rope pulling them onto the beach as fast as he could. Brea was fascinated and tried to observe more of the surrounding area. This was not like The Neighborhood. There were many one story houses up past the beach, and further behind she thought there were a large row of three story homes. She also noticed that the rock wall had lanes carved into it. These sandy lanes were narrow, but each lane had a higher rock wall behind it. It kept growing taller until she could no longer see the top. Dillin ran over to the car, and Brea followed him.

"I'm getting in, pushing that button, and finally going for a ride!" said a lit up Dillin.

"You don't know how to drive," replied Brea.

"There's nothing to know! You push the button, step on the petal and go! My Grandfather has told me for years in notes," replied Dillin.

"Well, I'm not getting into that thing! You couldn't get me inside of that gizmo for anything!"

"Okay, but I'm going. You stay here and I'll be back," said Dillin.

He got in and drove away leaving Brea standing on the beach. The sun was going to come up soon, and she ran to the rock wall to hide herself. She crept along the wall viewing the car as long as she could. Soon, the red car wasn't in sight anymore. Realizing she couldn't see Dillin anywhere, she began to feel uneasy. Suddenly, she bumped into another person. Brea turned, and was looking into the chest of someone in a red shirt and black jacket. She looked up, and there stood a tall young man with brownish blonde hair and blue eyes staring down at her.

"I saw the lights from your boat and came down to the beach. You are not a Container. Who are you?" said and asked the stranger in a whisper.

"No. I'm not a Container." replied Brea.

"Where are you from? Just tell me that."

"I'm from The Neighborhood," answered Brea.

"Oh, Shit!" the young man cursed under his breath and continued to speak in a soft voice. "Stay right here. Don't move, and I'll be right back, understand?"

Brea nodded her head, and he took off running. Confused didn't begin to explain how she felt, but he was back in a few minutes with a great big blanket.

"Put this around you, and follow me," said the young man.

"But my friend. I don't know where he is, and I can't just leave him," replied Brea.

"You mean, you can't do to him what he did to you?" he asked and continued to speak to her, "I know whose car that is that he stole, and already let him know. Let's just hope Tamron finds him before someone else does. Now, come on before someone sees you, too!"

Brea followed the young man, and he took care that no one saw them enter his house. It was very nice, but unusual to her because it was only one story. Before going inside, she noticed many of these one story houses. They were built on small foundations with two steps leading into the dwelling. They were erected on top of the grass that ended not far from the sandy beach. And she was right about the three story homes. They were resting on hillsides in the distance. Bizarre. That was the one word to describe this place.

"Have a seat, and by the way, my name is Ren," he said.

"I'm Brea, and my friend's name is Dillin," she replied.

"Well Brea, where does your friend get off stealing my friend's car?" asked Ren.

"He doesn't know any better. He was so excited to see one," explained Brea.

"How does he even know what a car is?" he asked.

"His Grandfather has been showing him pictures and telling him about them for years."

"That's just perfect! Do you have any idea how much trouble the two of you could be in? I have to go down to the beach and hide your boat before sunrise. Don't leave my home. When Tamron finds your friend, he knows to bring him here, and hopefully he'll find him before anyone else does. If you're hungry, help yourself to some food, and try not to burn my house down!" said the angry young man.

Ren didn't give Brea a moment to answer him back. He was up and out the door in a second. She sat where she was for a few minutes, and then got up to see what he had to eat. Her leg hurt, and she limped as she walked. Why was she noticing this only now? Brea doubted this Ren guy would even care and hobbled over to his fridge. She got a bottle of water, some cheese, and meat. She sat in a chair and ate. It was good, but Brea was wet, full of sand, and felt filthy. After eating, Brea started to hear soft noises coming from the other part of the living room. She crossed over to the sounds and came to a big box. Inside was the most beautiful dog she had ever seen, and four tiny little ones that were marked and colored almost exactly like her!

Chapter Ten

As Brea watched the dog and her babies, she wanted to reach in and pet one. She didn't know if she should, but a couple of the babies had moved away from their mother, and so she reached inside to pet one. The mother started to show its teeth and make a scary sound in her direction. Brea backed away but kept watching them. She could not take her eyes off these dogs. The mom was so gorgeous, and her babies were absolutely adorable. This kept Brea's mind and attention occupied while she waited for Dillin to come back and getting her bearings in these new surroundings.

The next thing she knew, the front door swung open with a bang, and in came Ren holding both of their backpacks, a guy with red hair and brown eyes that she supposed was Tamron, and he was carrying Dillin wrapped up in a blanket. Dillin was badly injured, and Brea could tell by looking at his face. He was grimacing and trying to hold back tears. Brea was on her feet and across to Dillin immediately.

"What happened?" asked Brea.

"Your idiot friend stole my car and flipped it! He better be grateful he's already hurt, or I would have hurt this character much worse than he is now!" yelled Tamron, and then looked at Ren and asked, "Do you have any adhesive?

"No. I'm out," he replied.

"We can't stitch him up because he's from The Neighborhood. Hope I have enough at my house," said Tamron.

"I got the rest. Bandages, ointment, and antibiotics," replied Ren.

"Ya know, you two have a lot of balls coming here! And today of all days. Damn it!" said Tamron looking right at Brea.

He slammed the door and was gone. Dillin was moaning on the floor, but Ren asked Brea to come away and sit down.

"What did he mean by "balls"? asked Brea.

"Nerve. He meant you had a lot of nerve coming here," said Ren and asked, "How did you get here?"

Brea told him the whole story and didn't leave out anything. Ren listened to her and was floored! They made it down the rapids? They saw a Solar Hunting Flyer, and the people covered in mud? He thought to himself that they had to get these two outta here as soon as possible before they found out anything else. But how? People were soon to be getting up. It was Ritual Day. What the hell was he going to do? Dillin started to yell in pain. They both went over to him, and Ren pulled back the blanket. Brea shrieked when she saw his blood. She was not used to the sight of it, but the wrap Tamron put on Dillin's arm was not sufficient. His arm, shirt, and pants were covered in blood.

"What are you going to do for him?" asked Brea.

Ren was already going for a thick cloth. He came back and unwrapped the one seeping in red, and they both saw how deep the cut was on his arm.

"He's going to bleed to death!" yelled Brea.

"No, he won't. If you can't help, go sit down and keep quiet," said Ren.

"How can I help?" asked the scared girl.

"Keep his wound closed while I wrap it up in this cloth."

The mere thought of touching his wound made her shiver visibly, and she got up and sat down in a chair. Tamron came in moments later, and both young men went to work on Dillin. Ren kept the wound closed, and Tamron took this clear thick liquid and spread it down the length of the cut. Then Ren handed Tamron a needle.

"What's that?" asked Brea.

"It's for infection. He doesn't need to get a fever on top of the wound," replied Ren.

Once the adhesive was dry, Ren wrapped the wound up in clean bandages. Tamron had a bottle of water and a pill that he told Dillin to swallow.

"And I'm taking this pill for what reason?" Dillin asked weakly.

"It's for the pain. Take it," answered Ren.

"That's about all we can do. I have to go and start preparing for this afternoon, and you should too," said Tamron.

"Have to stay here and keep an eye on them," replied Ren.

"What are we gonna do?" asked Tamron.

"There's nothing we can do until tonight. We have to be okay with the fact that no one else has seen them but us and keep it that way no matter what."

"This is bull! They can't stay for our Ritual Day!" said Tamron.

"Oh, you call Promotion Day a Ritual Day, here?" asked Brea.

"Hells Bells! This is NUTS!" yelled Tamron.

"You can lose it all you want, but it's the only way. I got their boat covered, and they just have to stay inside while it's going on," replied Ren.

Tamron just shook his head and looked at Brea and Dillin like he could slap both of them senseless.

"Hey! I don't want to be anywhere I'm not wanted. I'll just go," said Brea.

"NO!" both Tamron and Ren yelled at the same time.

"It's not safe for you out there," said Ren.

"It doesn't seem safe in here either," replied Brea.

"Damn these two dopes! Rennet, try to explain it to them. I gotta go, but don't worry. I'll cover for you."

On that note, Tamron left slamming the door even harder. The noise made Dillin wince, and Brea got up and asked him if he was okay. He just shrugged and looked at her with hazy eyes.

"Why did he call you Rennet?" asked Brea.

"That's my given name, but I only hear Rennet when someone is mad at me. Most of the time, people call me Ren for short," said the young man and asked, "Can you help me get him to the couch with that leg of yours?"

"I don't know. Is there anything you can do for my leg?"

He left the room and came back with a square blue bag.

"What's this?" asked Brea.

"You don't know anything, do you? It's an ice pack. Put it where you're in pain, and it will help."

"I know plenty where I'm from but stop treating me like a simpleton for not knowing about this place," said Brea.

"Okay. That's fair. Is there anything else I can do for you?" asked a sarcastic Ren.

"Yes, there is. You have a dog, and she has babies. May I hold one?" answered and asked an innocent sounding Brea.

"Do you have any idea how much we are doing for the two of you, already?" questioned Ren and went on, "We are keeping your presence unknown to our own Territory. Tamron will take the blame and be teased for what your friend did to his car, your boat is hidden in a safe place, and we have sealed and treated the wounds of you both."

"You're right, you have. I'm sorry. Thank you," said Brea in earnest.

"Anyway, those are not called babies. They are her puppies, and my dog is named Summer. I named her after this Grove we live in," replied the young man.

"I thought you were Containers," said Brea.

"Yes. This is The Container Territory. You live in The Neighborhood Territory, and there are three more Territories that make up Summer Grove," explained Ren.

Brea thought she kinda understood and asked, "Are the Invisible Healers one of the Territories here?"

"Very good. Yes, they are, but we are given a certain amount of medical education and training, and only call them in a real emergency," said Ren.

"Wow. I could never do what you guys did. It was incredible. Really," replied Brea.

"You could if you were raised like us."

Ren went to the box and got a puppy. He handed the tiny ball of fur out to Brea, and she wiggled and smiled so brightly he couldn't relate to her reaction because dogs were common in his Territory. Brea petted this small little thing, and the feeling of this puppy made her feel inexplicably warm inside. She lifted the puppy to her face, and the animal licked her. This was the most precious feeling, and his breath smelled like fresh cut baloney!

"So, what do you contain here?" asked Brea.

"You already know. You saw the day you got to the partial clearing. By the way, that must have taken you guys hours to get there," replied Ren.

"Yup. It was quite a hike, but are you talking about those people covered in mud?" asked Brea.

"They are not people. They are Fodder, and responsible for most of the problems that were in this part of the world," replied Ren.

"I don't understand. They looked like people to me. Only, they were extremely dirty," said Brea.

"Well, they're not people. They're Fodder. The word person or human is not applied to those animals. The official word for those things is Fodder. Our Grandparents started this work, it was passed on to our parents, and now that we are eighteen it will be decided what we are going to do. First, we are given about nine months to reside here rule free on the beach. That's why we're not in the hills with our families. We are allowed this time to spend together before the rest of our lives is chosen for us," explained Ren.

"I wish we got something like that before Promotion Day, and becoming an Elite," said a wistful Brea.

Ren burst out laughing and couldn't stop. He was holding his stomach and laughing so hard it was making Brea uncomfortable for some unknown reason.

"I don't know which is worse, being yelled at by you two, or being laughed at!" spat Brea.

Ren controlled his laughter and said: "You, Dillin, and everyone in The Neighborhood are not being raised and trained to be picked on Promotion Day to be an Elite. You are being groomed to SERVE The Elites."

Brea was stunned, and the only word she could get to come out of her mouth was, "What?"

"Oh yeah, you're the servant class for The Elites. That's why you have to learn languages and etiquette. The Neighborhood is where they get the best in service and entertainment."

Brea's jaw dropped. It was the first time in her life she was rendered speechless.

"Do you think you can help me get Dillin on the couch? I'll show you both something to explain it better," asked and said Ren as he pointed to a massive black screen on his wall.

They worked together, but Brea was still trying to process what he had told her. She took his legs, and Ren wrapped his arms around his back. It took a while because Dillin would loudly moan, and Brea couldn't handle the sounds of pain coming from his throat. It scared her, and she thought they were hurting him. After they had him on the carpet by the couch, Ren cleaned up the blood on the floor in his hallway. Brea couldn't bear to watch. She picked up the puppy and played with it until he was done. They walked over to Dillin knowing they only had to lift him on the couch, and he would be much more comfortable.

Chapter Eleven

Once they had Dillin laid on one of his couches, Ren turned on his screen, and told Brea and Dillin to watch and learn. The three of them watched what Brea could only describe as a presentation of the old days, how the world used to be, and what it's like today. They saw scenes of what they called Fodder running through the streets, throwing rocks, bricks, glass bottles, and devices that exploded when tossed at white people on the other side of fences. There were metal machines that both sides had that made very loud noises. When these machines were pulled, some other kind of small metal came out of them and if they hit a person blood came out of them. People were falling to the ground and bleeding. They saw other people dressed in protective gear shooting back, and they were white. Ren informed them that these metal weapons were called guns, but there was no need for them any longer.

They saw how crowded everyone was. They saw how dirty everyone, and everything was, and it did not escape Brea's notice that some of these people on the Fodder's side were white. Then came images of how muddy the rivers were, the oceans filled with metal, glass, and something called plastic, and how disgusting and polluted the air was from this black smoke rising from buildings all over the world. To contrast this, scenes were shown side by side to illustrate what the world looked like before and after. These same rivers that looked like mud were now crystal clean, the oceans were pristine, and so were the lakes. The fish and mammals that inhabited these many types of waters were no longer washed ashore dead or dying. They were thriving.

And the air! What a difference in the air. Before and after shots of filthy air that a person could hardly see through were shown, and then shots of the same place where anyone could see for miles instead of blocks. No more black smoke. No more of what were called air quality drills were needed. Because of these changes, the sun was no longer a threat, either. On this massive screen, Brea and Dillin learned that in some countries people had to wear large hats and wear lotion on their bodies to protect themselves from the sun. The sun was also destroying ocean reefs where oxygen was made, and animals lived, but through cleaner air and water this had been reversed. This one voice that talked over the entire presentation made it plain that The Elites had paid for this and made it all possible.

As they watched their world being cleaned up, Brea saw that it was regular people doing the work. Yeah, maybe The Elites paid for it, but it was clear to her that it was her Grandparents, Dillin's Grandparents, Lindy's Grandparents, and Ren and Tamron's Grandparents that made this regenerated world possible. She knew it. She knew it without a doubt. No matter how much The Elites took credit, it was that generation that had truly made it possible. She felt humbled and almost started to cry when she thought about the accomplishments of her Grandmother's life. It was swelling up in her throat, and almost spilled through her eyes. No wonder the Grandparents stayed on their Headgear! It was probably the most satisfying and significant part of their lives, and they got to replay it just as she got to replay the enjoyable parts of her life on her personal screen.

Then the man said something that stopped these feelings abruptly. He ended by saying none of this would have been possible without the containment of The Fodder. The Fodder in every part of the world were to blame for every problem, and everyone was never to forget that. Her body went cold. She felt the hair on the back of her neck rise, and a feeling in her gut was gnawing at her. How could this possibly be true? It wasn't. This was a lie.

When it was over, Ren shut off his screen, looked over at Brea and Dillin and said, "I thought watching this would be better than trying to explain it to you both. I could have shown you two another about the wars of the past but thought that would be too much in one day."

"What's a war?" asked Brea.

"Terrible death and destruction. Misery and suffering on a massive scale with weapons too horrible to describe. We did away with that too. There were many that didn't like giving up their guns or war powers, but they had no choice. This is The Elites world now," said Ren.

"So, you think what you do with Fodder is different?" asked Brea.

"You're damn right it is! The Fodder is the reason for every single problem in this part of the world, and we are the ones that deal with them. You don't, and you don't know half of what we go through!" answered Ren forcefully.

"No, I don't, and don't want to know about this thing you call war. There are a couple of things about my Neighborhood I would like to know," said Brea.

"Oh crap! Here we go," said Dillin.

"Yes, here we go. We will never have another opportunity to find out, and so I'm going to ask. Ren seems to know everything about this place called Summer Grove. If he can tell us the truth about The Neighborhood, why not ask?"

"What do you want to know?" asked Ren.

"Two things. Why don't we know about the lake at the end of our Neighborhood, and what goes on in the last four occupied houses?"

Ren grabbed a comfy chair and pulled it in front of Dillin and Brea and got settled. He took a deep breath and began.

Chapter Twelve

"First of all, not everyone in The Dining part of The Neighborhood knows about the lake. There is a special society of people who have always lived in separate housing apart from the others. You might say that The Dining Specialty is split in two different departments. The ones that are secret are trained to be fisherman, others to gut and wrap the fish, still more to help with loading and unloading the trucks that come in with food and other items from other Territories, and still others that are the workers in every Specialty grocery store. How do you think you get your food, clothes, and other supplies? It all happens there in that separate part of your Neighborhood," explained Ren.

"I always wondered where our food and stuff came from," said Brea.

"Like that's a surprise! She wonders about everything," Dillin told Ren.

"I have no doubt. Anyway, you know those buttons you push to go to your Socials?" asked Ren.

They both nodded their heads, and Ren continued on.

"Those buttons are used to transport everything to your grocery stores on the first lower floor at night. They are packaged up and labeled by

Specialty, and everyone gets what they need from clothes to food to blankets, and anything that has to do with their part of The Neighborhood. That's how it happens," finished Ren with his explanation.

"Are you satisfied? Because it makes a lot of sense to me. It's also the reason we didn't recognize anyone last night," said Dillin as he was looking at and speaking to Brea.

"Yes, I am. This means there are secrets at the beginning of our Neighborhood, and at the end of it. Isn't that correct, Ren?"

"Yeah, that's right," responded the young man.

"Will you tell us what goes on in those last four occupied houses?" asked Brea.

"You might not like the answer. Think about it," replied Ren.

"Nothing will change her mind, Ren. She's been wanting to know forever," chimed in Dillin.

She paid no mind to Dillin's remark and said, "I want to know, and if you can tell us, go on."

"Dillin, you don't have to hear about this. You can go into one of my bedrooms," said Ren.

"No. If she's gonna hear about it, I want to hear it with her," he answered back.

"Okay. In every Neighborhood Territory all over the world there are three to six houses that are just like the one in yours. No one goes in or out, and they are trained for two different Specialties. In our hemisphere, the color painted on the outside of the homes signifies Erotica. You two had sex education in school, right?

While Brea started stroking the puppy in her lap a little faster, she replied, "Yes. We are taught about it in basic science."

"They are taught from a very young age how to give sexual pleasure to The Elites. They start learning young at around the age of four years old. They can be bought by the age of six years old. They are taught by people in different families, and every floor has a different family. They are bred to be sex slaves, and they are the only Specialty that The Elites must pay money for," explained Ren.

"Sex Slaves? Are you serious?" asked Brea with a voice filled with distress.

"Just listen. You wanted to know about this. Don't interrupt. There are men and women within the population of The Elites that are willing to pay huge amounts of money for children and teenagers to give them sexual pleasure. There is a small percentage of them that have sexual appetites that are not conventional. Some men desire little boys, and some that desire little girls. There are women that desire the same. There are others that desire teenagers, and they are willing to pay a premium price to have them and leave their own Elite children untouched," finished Ren.

Brea was trying to fight off this queasy feeling in her stomach coupled with dizziness, but still managed to ask, "You mean little babies are being touched constantly in their private parts for these monsters we call The Elites?"

Ren's reply was soft and low, "Yes, Brea."

Her response was immediate. She got up with the puppy in her arms, laid him on the chair, and then ran into Ren's bathroom where she heaved her guts out for around twenty minutes. When nothing else was left to come up, she stayed on her knees and cried her eyes out for those unknown children and teenagers. In the meantime, Dillin and Ren were having a conversation of their own after Brea screamed at them to leave her alone.

"Dillin, was this too much for her?" asked Ren.

"Apparently, she's having a pretty bad reaction to this news, but Brea is the strongest person I've come across. She'll be okay," replied Dillin, and added, "It was tough for me to hear."

"I'm sure, but you're not throwing up in my bathroom. How can you be so certain? About Brea?" asked Ren.

"Because her dad was taken away years ago, and she handled that. She loved and adored her father, and I know it broke her heart. She never shows it, though. She comforts herself with the knowledge that her dad is a Doctor. We know now that he's not an Elite, but he's got more choices than any of us."

"That's unusual, but not unheard of, and maybe that's why she needs to know everything," said Ren.

"I don't follow you," replied Dillin.

"Maybe she's trying to find out everything thinking she might find her dad," he said.

"No. She's been like this since I met her when we were four, but maybe her dad being taken intensified it," replied Dillin.

"You know her much better than I do, but I am worried for her," said Ren.

"Don't be. What you told us is pretty repulsive," stated Dillin.

"That's true, but people are weird in The Elites. Some are stranger than others, and that's why they go out of their way to keep that Specialty as secret as they can. I think they do a pretty good job."

"I think they do an excellent job. Unfortunately, we're here finding out about it," said Dillin.

Around this time, Brea emerged from the bathroom, sat on the floor beside Dillin where he was laying on the couch and held his hand. She looked into his eyes and shook her head.

"The Elites are disgusting!" she said.

Ren replied somewhat annoyed, "Wait a minute. I'm not talking about all of them. It's a very low percentage. Why do you think they are the smallest Specialty in every Neighborhood?"

"Let me ask you something. When they are done with these kids and teenagers, what happens to them?" asked Brea.

"That's where their second Specialty comes in. They are also trained to be cooks, maids, and other kinds of servants for the Science and Medical Territories," explained Ren.

"So, they're trapped in despicable servitude their entire lives!" burst out Brea.

"So they are. So are you. So are we all."

Chapter Thirteen

Ren's comment rendered all three of them silent. Nobody said a word for a long time. Brea got up from the floor, picked up the puppy, sat back in the chair, and started petting the tiny warm thing once again. The sense of security from this animal wasn't something she could describe, but this ball of fur was the only thing she had to give her comfort after the news about The Neighborhood. She was trying to decide if she felt better or worse about knowing what went on in those last four houses. It was revolting to her, and she believed it was wrong. If it weren't, The Elites would do these terrible things to their own children, and they surely wouldn't pay any of their precious money for them. Still, she didn't regret being told. Brea decided that it was better to know and went back to the pleasure and warmth the puppy provided.

Dillin laid on the couch thinking about how until today he had figured his life was his own. That was a fallacy. He belonged to nameless faceless people who were grooming him to serve them. That he was being groomed in better circumstances than the people from the past didn't matter. Actually, between what his Grandfather had been relaying to him, and what he found out today was solidifying an idea. It wasn't just that the people from the old days had more things. No, it was more than that. He got a sense that those individuals had more choices in the way they lived. He did not.

Ren was trying to decide if he had made a mistake in telling these two strangers any part of the truth. He knew The Elites wanted them in the dark about their circumstances, and he had told them things he shouldn't. He knew he did right by concealing them from the others, but for them to show up today of all days. He had to get them out of here, but Dillin needed rest. He and Tamron would be able to help them get back home, but only after dark. It would be much later because of The Ritual. How was he going to keep them away from that? After what seemed to be a lifetime, Dillin was the one who finally spoke first, but only because his arm was throbbing in pain.

"I feel awful," he said.

"I'll go get you a pill for sleep with a glass of water. Be right back," replied Ren.

After he left the room, Dillin looked at Brea and asked, "How am I supposed to go home with blood all over my clothes?"

"You have a change of clothes, and you'll dress in them when we go back."

"What do I say about an entire outfit of mine missing?"

Brea didn't have the answer to that and asked Ren what they could do about his clothes when he came back. He instructed Dillin to give him the clothes and he would clean them. The Containers knew how to get blood stains off of anything. The two young men went back into Ren's bedroom with him steadying Dillin as they walked. When they got back, Dillin was wearing a bright orange Container shirt, and his own extra pair of jeans. Once he was settled back on the couch, Ren handed him the glass of water and the pill. Dillin took the medicine and thanked him for his help.

"No problem. You'll be asleep soon, and when you wake up you'll be feeling better," replied Ren.

"How do you know he'll feel better?" asked Brea.

"Because our bodies heal faster when we sleep."

Within five minutes, Dillin was snoring away on the couch.

"Well, you were right about that. Dillin is knocked out," said Brea.

"And he will be asleep for about three hours," said Ren.

Brea kept a hold of the puppy. She held him to her neck, and he climbed further up a bit, licking her face. These are little puppy kisses she thought to herself. He was the sweetest thing she had held in her life.

Ren watched her for a few minutes and then asked her, "Is this what you want to do for the next three hours?"

"I wouldn't mind. Can't have a puppy in The Neighborhood and holding him is pleasing in so many ways. Plus, you said it's dangerous for us out there," replied Brea.

"It is, but I have an old bodysuit from when I was younger and think it will fit you. Change into it, put up your hair and cover it with one of my hats, and I'll take you for a ride," said Ren.

"What kind of ride?" asked Brea, getting a little excited and nervous at the same time.

"Before you two went down the rapids, did you like being in a boat?"

"Yeah, until then, I liked it a lot," answered Brea.

"Right. Get changed, and I'll take you for a ride on my speedboat. I'll take you out on the ocean beyond the waves. It's great out there, and I think you'll have a good time," said Ren.

"Sounds good to me but will Dillin be okay?" asked Brea.

"Sure. He'll be fine. If it makes you feel better, I'll have Tamron look in on him," replied Ren.

Brea took Ren's old clothes and hat. She took a quick shower and changed in his bathroom. This bodysuit had short sleeves, was lightweight, comfortable, but a terrible color of yellow. It was like wearing nothing, but her entire body was covered. She came out of the room, and they took off for his speedboat. They had to walk along the edge of the great wall that was close to his house. Brea was thankful for that because they wouldn't be seen by anyone. She did see a few Containers in a couple of the isles that were cut out of the rock wall, but they were coming in from the ocean, and putting away their sea toys. Ren told her that because today was their

Ritual Day, people were getting in their play time much earlier. Brea didn't understand but nodded her head as if she did.

About five rows down, Ren turned left, and Brea followed. They ended up at a wooden walkway with boats along both sides. They were kept in place by rope that was placed from the boat and wrapped around a metal ball. Ren got into one of these boats and held out his hand for Brea to take. She climbed in and Ren told her to hang on to the railing. She did and he pushed a bright yellow button in the shape of the sun. It started up the boat, and he slowly pulled the boat away. As they got beyond the waves, he picked up speed. He looked over at Brea to see if she was scared, but she was smiling, the hat was gone, and her long blonde hair was blowing in the wind. Ren pushed another button, and the boat started going full speed. She felt as if they were streaking across the ocean as fast as a bolt of lightning flashes across the sky. Brea had never felt so exhilarated as she did during this new experience.

Chapter Fourteen

When Ren slowed the boat to a stop, they both sat down, and were breathless.

"I thought any second we were going to fly into the air! What an amazing feeling!" cried Brea.

"Yeah, I love going out on my boat at full speed. It clears my head and makes me feel totally free," replied Ren.

"I can see that. Wish we had boats like this in The Neighborhood."

"There's more to do out here besides going fast."

Ren pressed another button, and the bottom slid back revealing the ocean underneath them. Brea could see straight down to the ocean floor through the thick glass. In about a minute, she saw a bunch of brightly colored fish go by.

"I've never seen anything like this. How beautiful they are," exclaimed Brea.

"Yeah, they are. Aren't they? And there is so much more. Keep looking," replied Ren.

As the two of them floated along, Brea saw beautiful ocean flowers and other fish that she didn't ask questions about. She just wanted to look and keep watching for the next thing that set her mind full of wonderful emotions. It was so calming out here. She was feeling that beautiful, quiet, and soothing sensation for a second time. Abruptly, she was jolted up by a noise. Something was rising out of the ocean and making the loveliest sounds. They were blue creatures, blowing air from the top of their heads, and flipping into the air!

"What are those?' asked Brea in total fascination.

"They're Dolphins, and one of the smartest mammals on this planet. They are curious and friendly when it comes to humans. Don't be afraid," explained Ren.

"I don't know what to say," said Brea in a voice so soft Ren could hardly hear her.

Then both of them watched as the two Dolphins swam around the boat, jumped high into the air, and one of them put their head on the edge of the boat making whistling sounds that Brea could only guess was Dolphin language. She was thoroughly entranced by these water creatures. She reached out to touch the Dolphin, but it jumped back into the sea. The two Dolphins stayed for a time, but after about ten minutes they swam away.

"Oh No! Come back to us!" cried Brea.

Ren laughed and said, "You can't call them back. They come and go as they please. You're lucky to have seen them at all."

"Lucky? What's lucky?"

"That's right. You say Good Fortune in The Neighborhood. Here we say Good Luck, or hope we get lucky."

"I still don't understand," replied Brea.

"In The Neighborhood, you all have it made. You either get promoted, become a teacher of children, an assistant coach, or get married. If you are from here, nothing is decided on skill. Nine months after we turn eighteen, our names are thrown into a large whirling glass barrel. They call out the area, and then names are drawn out of it. If the area is the Space Station, that's where you go. If it's Hunting, that's it. You're a hunter. If it's Containment, you're on Containment Detail. If your name is drawn for Breeding, you're a breeder, and you get married. So, we wish each other Luck. The luck of the drawing."

"I think I understand. You are taught all of it, and it's left to a draw," replied Brea.

"Yes, just like you are, but your choices don't carry the responsibilities of our Territory. You live your lives completely unaware of what goes on in other parts of the Territories," said Ren.

"I haven't been trained in every part of my Specialty," said Brea.

"Sure, you have. You know enough about your Specialty to be an assistant coach. You learned how to cook, clean, and wash clothes in the basics of your etiquette classes if you are picked to be a parent. You'd have your mom to help you with any babies you may have and are smart enough to teach the young ones. Am I right or not?"

"I guess that's true, but I didn't suppose I'd be anything other than promoted. I'm ranked number one in my Specialty."

"But you didn't get promoted even though you are a Gaming Master?" asked Ren.

"No, and neither did Dillin. He's a Master too."

"But you do see that your Territory is different, and you have no need to wish on yourself or anyone else the element of luck?"

"Yeah, I do. Ren, if you did have a choice, what would you want to be?" asked Brea.

"Well, I have no interest in being in space as a mechanic, or on Containment Detail. I don't think I would make a good father, and so I would like to be a Hunter."

Brea was perplexed, and asked, "Why would you want to chase and capture those poor people?"

"They're not people. They are Fodder. They are not like us, and never have been," Ren said, but he was not angry. It was more of a cold definition about them.

"Okay Ren, I'll call them Fodder, but do you really believe that they are not people like you and me?" asked Brea.

"I believe in what my Territory stands for, and the peace and stability it maintains throughout every Grove in this part of the world. And yes, I want to be a Hunter, but not for the reasons you might think. Not everyone my age is comfortable with everything that goes on here. I would be an extremely ineffective Hunter."

All of a sudden, Brea thought about her dad, and a sinking feeling wrapped itself around her heart.

Observing the change in her face and body language he asked, "What's wrong?"

"My father was taken away by The Elites when I was almost nine. We were told he was removed to be a doctor. I've always thought he was an Elite, but I guess he isn't," said Brea.

"Dillin told me about that earlier today. Your dad has the best life of anyone born outside The Elite Class. I remember that time, now. There was a shortage of doctors, and they went through tons of files on people from every Territory looking for anyone who qualified in science. Your dad may not be an Elite, but he's the closest any of us ever get. Brea, you can still be happy and proud of him," replied Ren.

Brea was feeling dizzy and confused, once more. Too much information, and a lot of it wasn't pleasant. She put her thoughts about her dad aside and asked Ren another question before she lost her nerve. She was afraid but didn't know why.

"Explain to me why you would want to be a Hunter?" asked an edgy Brea.

"If I get lucky and chosen to be a Hunter, I will train in one of those solar hunting flyers, but eventually I'll get a flyer of my own and pick my own crew. People that believe like I do. We wouldn't be delivering many Fodder to Container Detail," said Ren.

"Then why don't you try stopping this? You and the others that believe like you do?" asked Brea.

"There aren't enough of us. There are Container Territories all over the world. Other Groves have their own kinds of Fodder. The Elites have this completely under their control. Brea, I can only do what I can do," responded Ren in a defeatist tone.

"It isn't fair. Millions upon millions of people worked together to save this world, and what did they get in return? Too many were thanked by being killed. Many of them were what you now call fodder, and many were as white as you and me," said Brea.

"But The Fodder were the ones that caused all the trouble. The white people that took their side were misled and confused, but they were given a chance to choose," replied Ren.

"Yeah, okay. You're told that, but do you really believe it? You must have doubts, or you'd be on board with everything that goes on here. Until yesterday, I believed that I was training to become an Elite. Today I found out that I'm just gonna be some glorified servant."

"Brea, you still have no idea how lucky you are. I'd give anything to have your advantages. We all have certain ones, but The Neighborhoods have the most. What The Elites knew was if you satisfied people's basic needs with good food, a nice place to live, and something to do with their lives with no pressure they would be contented," said Ren.

"Say that's true. You aren't bothered by the fact that The Elites selected who got to have that kind of life? And by the way, I'd love to have a dog of my own, a car, a boat like yours, and almost a year away from certain members of my family."

Ren responded, "You really are something! Most people died from those viruses, and the undesirables from other parts of the world released them. The Fodder here were the ones who caught and spread those plagues more than anything else did. And for your information, these toys, my dog, and our nine months of freedom is our compensation for dealing with reality. For being The Containers and keeping the world safe. Why do you think that barrier is up miles and miles away from your homes? It's so you never have to deal with the Fodder and are never bothered or terrorized by them."

Brea thought about Ren's last statement for a few minutes, and she could see the strain on his face and in his eyes.

Brea said carefully, "I'm sorry you have this burden, but I still think there's something off here. The world is safe. The world is clean. Why can't we all have this stuff? Why can't we all share? And why is it that only The Elites have money?"

"In the old days, many had their money and property taken from them. It was determined that most people weren't to be trusted with money. They misused it, and only the professionals could be trusted with currency. You have no idea the pressure that comes from having money, or not enough of it. The old times were filled with so many that didn't have enough money. It was called poverty, and the pressure of providing for a family was constant. There were also the ones who had money but wasted it. Athletes used to be paid millions of dollars to play sports. Now, they are trained in The Neighborhoods, and play for free for The Elites. The same goes for singers, actors, musicians, painters, chefs, dancers and even you gamers. You all live comfortably, are treated with respect in your field, but there is no money or getting out of it once you're promoted. Even some of The Fodder had money and property that was taken away from them in the old times," explained Ren.

He relayed this to her as if it were nothing. No big deal. Brea felt peculiar and wanted to go home. Ren tried to answer her questions, but something kept tugging at her that he was either lying to her or being lied to. She wished she and Dillin never came here, but this is what she asked for. She wanted answers to her questions, but this was too much. Ren started up the speedboat and told her they had to get back. Brea nodded her head, and they were back at his house before she knew it.

Chapter Fifteen

Dillin was awake on their return to the house and said, "I ain't feelin' so hot."

Ren replied, "You ain't lookin so hot, either. I'm gonna get you some water and change your bandage."

Some of Dillin's blood was seeping through the bandages and Ren, knowing neither of these guys from The Neighborhood were used to seeing blood, got to work on what he thought was the real problem. Tamron had done an excellent job of closing the cut with the adhesive, but Ren wanted to change the bandage, get rid of the sight of the blood, and set their minds at ease. He could put more adhesive on the cut, too.

When Ren left the room, Dillin asked, "Brea, where did you go?"

"You had your car ride, and I had an ocean ride. I went on something called a speedboat, and Ren took me out beyond the waves. It was beautiful out there, and I don't think I'll ever forget it," replied Brea.

"You had a good time?" asked Dillin.

"For the most part, but I also learned some things. Some of it was quite disturbing, and I don't think I fully understand. My equilibrium has done a 180. I feel like I'm standing on my head instead of my feet."

Dillin replied, "I kinda feel that same way, but pretty sure my condition is because of the car accident, and I think the pill Ren gave me for pain has made me feel off balance."

Brea couldn't help herself and laughed, saying, "Well, that's what you get for taking a car that didn't belong to you!"

Dillin sighed, "I know, but just couldn't help myself. Driving a car is what I've been dreaming about for years, and I finally saw my chance. Really sorry I put on the brakes in shallow water and flipped the thing. Thankfully, the car flipped over twice and landed right. I did damage it, though. I'm not surprised Tamron didn't pound me."

"He didn't need to! Look at you! You're a mess. The cut down your arm, the bruises all over, and you were bleeding a lot."

Ren came back with a bottle of water, the thick adhesive, and the bandages. He changed the dressing on Dillin's arm and handed him a blue bag.

"What's this?" asked Dillin.

"It's an ice bag, and it will help with your swelling," said Brea.

Dillin stared at her and started to say something, but Brea interrupted him with more words.

"Ren gave me one earlier for my leg. It helps a lot. Try it."

The ice bag was applied, and it did feel instantly cooler. It was much better than ice cubes in a cloth. It was numbing the pain of his bruises faster. Ren informed them Dillin's clothes were clean, and he put them back in his pack. The door opened, and Tamron walked in. He sat down in a chair, looked at the three of them, and then let out a huff.

"What?" asked Ren.

"What do you mean, what? These two are a problem. Rennet, Can't you get that through your thick skull? We gotta go!"

"I guess he's pissed off at you again," said Brea.

"You bet I am! You take her for a ride and let me cover for you?" said and asked Tamron.

"You're right. Sorry, but I got bored. There's not much left to do, and they both have to stay here until it's over," said Ren.

"We can't see?" asked Brea.

"No! In about 30 minutes it's gonna start, and we can't take any chances with you two," replied Tamron.

Ren jumped in saying, "You're gonna have to stay here until at least midnight, and then we'll help you and Dillin get back into your boat to go home."

Brea responded with a question, "That's the only way?"

Ren and Tamron said, "YES!" in unison and with much irritation.

"This is too dangerous. You two stay here. Rennet, you force them to understand," said Tamron.

Ren nodded in agreement.

Tamron approached his friend, placed a hand on his shoulder, and said, "Sorry Ren. See you in a few."

"Don't worry. I'll explain it to them, and be right there," replied Ren.

Tamron said goodbye to Brea and Dillin and he hurried out the door.

Brea spoke up weakly, "Okay Ren, tell us whatever it is that we are supposed to understand now."

Ren walked over to a drawer and opened it. He pulled out what looked to be Headgear, but they were too small. He called them: Headsets. They still had big earmuffs, but just a band of metal across the head. He put them both on the couch beside Dillin.

"While The Ritual is going on, I want you both to wear these headsets, and don't go near the window. Don't look. I don't care what happens, or what you think you might see through the blinds. You are not to look outside. Is that clear?" Ren said and asked them both.

"You're not gonna get any problem from me, but I can't speak for her," answered Dillin while looking over at Brea.

"Brea, for once in your life just stay put!" said Ren.

"I don't know if I can," she answered in a teasing tone.

"HEY! I'M NOT JOKING!" roared Ren.

"ME EITHER!" yelled back Brea.

Ren stared up at his ceiling and said, "Oh, DAMN IT! I give UP!"

"Tell me about it. She's been like this all her life," replied Dillin.

"Well, she better change fast," said Ren.

"Don't hold your breath," replied Dillin.

"Does she have a brick for brains?" asked Ren.

Brea, feeling ignored and angry, said, "I'm standing right here you two morons, and can hear everything you say! And it's not like I don't know how I am. So, since I'm such a problem, are you gonna tie me up and gag me?"

Ren said, "Of course not! Brea, I'm just telling you, and it's for your own good to mind your business! None of this is any of your concern! Can you do that? Please, put the headsets on, and don't go near the window. That's it. That's all!"

Ren stomped off out of his house, slammed his door on the way out, and left Brea and Dillin alone in his home with both of their mouths wide open.

"Well, that was pretty rude. Don't you think?" asked Brea.

"No. Actually, I don't. Will you please sit down and shut up for once in your life?" asked Dillin, and nothing but anger filled his voice.

Brea was astonished! In the thirteen years they had been friends, Dillin had never spoken to her in this way. She sat down.

"I know you. I know your good points and admire your strengths. Your insatiable curiosity is a pain at times, and it could get you hurt someday. Hurt more than you think, and I believe this is one of those times. We're in like another world, and Ren and Tamron have taken us in. They have protected us. Ren told us things he didn't have to, and now he's trying to shield us from something. Brea, I believe him. We shouldn't watch."

"On the way back from the ocean, I wished we were home and had never come here. Now, I don't know. You're just beat up and in pain. That's why you don't want to find out," said Brea.

"That's true, but it isn't why I'm agreeing with him. Maybe you haven't seen, learned, and done enough in one day, but I have. Whatever is gonna happen out there tonight, I could care less."

"You're acting like what we saw on that huge screen means nothing! Billions of people had to die so we all could serve over two Billion Nitwits and think it's some kind of prize! And those poor kids and teenagers. This is horrible, and you have no idea what Ren told me on the boat," said Brea.

"As far as whatever he told you, I don't care. Do you understand? Maybe today hasn't been overwhelming enough for you. You said it was, but you're wavering again. Yeah, what we saw on that screen is important, but it was the generation of our Grandparents that saved this world together. We did not destroy ourselves or the planet because of them. We owe them plenty of thanks, and they had no idea what was coming next."

"Maybe we didn't completely destroy the human race, but most of it," countered Brea.

"You know, arguing with you is not making me feel any better. But even though I'm in this bad a shape, I'm still happy I know what it feels like to drive a car at full speed. It was the thrill of my life," Dillin said, and had an actual full smile on his face.

Brea couldn't help it. In the middle of this argument, she burst out laughing and said, "You are THE biggest idiot I've ever known! Do you know that?"

Dillin said with his big silly grin still on his face, "Yup, that's true, but you still love me."

"Yes. I do. You weirdo."

"So, we're back to the original question. What are you gonna do?" asked Dillin.

"I don't know, but you're right. They both seemed adamant that we not listen or watch."

"Ya think?" asked a sarcastic Dillin.

Brea abruptly changed the subject and said, "Give me a pair of the headsets."

Dillin handed her a pair, and she put them on. She asked Dillin to talk to her, but she couldn't hear a thing. She took them off and asked if he would scream at her. Brea put them back on and could tell by the straining of his throat that he was yelling, but she could not hear a sound! That's how good these headsets were. She took them off and looked at Dillin.

"These things work, and they work damn good," said Brea.

"Know what? Between my arm, bruised body, and everything else that's happened today, I'm glad they work exactly like he told us. The headsets are going on, and I'm gonna sit right here and wait for the guys to come back," replied Dillin.

He picked out a comfortable chair, put on the headset, and closed his eyes. Brea kicked the chair to get his attention.

When he opened his eyes, and held up the muffs, Brea said, "Hey! Nothing has started yet. We still have awhile to talk."

"About what? Brea, I'm done talking," answered her exhausted friend, and put the muffs back over his ears and closed his eyes.

Chapter Sixteen

She knew he had made his decision, and she was not going to mess with him about it. Plus, he was in awful shape, and she felt bad he was so banged up. Brea wanted to talk about her dad with Dillin, but she knew how smart he was and thought he had figured out what she had been slow to comprehend. Brea's dad was a doctor. He did have much more freedom and choices, but he was not an Elite. He worked for them. Exactly like she would if promoted next season. She had been deceived. What a farce. What a cruel joke. What a pack of lies. What a bunch of fools every single one of them were.

Brea also knew that they both had childhoods that were poles apart. He still had both of his parents and didn't have one of them yanked out of his family. Brea had, and survived it. She was able to tell her Aunt and Uncle to go "climb a tree" whenever she was forced into a situation with them, and they invariably brought up the subject of her dad. She was able to somewhat sympathize with her mom about this circumstance and tell her mom that they were insensitive creeps to bring him up in front of her. This probably wasn't enough support for her mom, but it was the best Brea could do.

Next, her thoughts couldn't help but trail back once more to the conversation she had with Ren on the boat, and children in the 4 last occupied houses in The Neighborhood. She didn't have a pleasant reaction to either of these conversations. It was only minutes ago that she didn't want to know anymore, and wished they were both home. She didn't understand why she was having such a hard time putting on the headset and staying away from the window. What was the quandary?

She heard music begin, and heard voices, too. It wasn't voices having conversations, but it was some kind of chanting. She didn't know what to make of this, and her mind began to reel. What could Ren and Tamron be so afraid of me seeing that could possibly be worse than finding out the truth about her dad, how this place operates, or about those poor little children? Nothing could top any of these things, and with that thought her mind was made up. Brea went to the window and opened the blinds wide enough so she could see outside. The sights outside were freakish, and that was saying something considering the experiences of this day.

She saw tall, large lights near the beach lit up around the area, and saw these people dancing around in a big, huge square. They had on brightly-colored costumes that were disturbing to her eyes. She didn't think she would ever get used to the bright reds, oranges, and yellows the people wore here. She liked the muted colors of The Neighborhood. The soft blues, ivories, and even the green colors. But anyway, there they were twirling around this square. They had precise steps to this dance. They spun around, dipped to their knees, grabbed a small piece of wood, and then threw it into the square. This was so different from her Promotion Day and wondered how Ren could compare the two.

As the music got louder, the chanting did too, but she still could not understand the words. She was too far away. More people started to gather to watch the dance as time went on, and a man stepped out to hand each of the dancers a stick. They held the stick high in the air at all times and used their other hand to throw pieces of wood into the square. Around this point, Brea concluded that these people were a pack of imbeciles! That's what they appeared to be to her. It started to get closer to late in the day, and she figured that's why they needed the big lights. They were supplied so everyone could watch this silly dance for as long as it lasted.

As they continued to dance around the large square, another man walked over with a lit torch. When each dancer went by this man, they extended their arm out to the man and the stick they were holding in the air was ignited, and everyone in the crowd yelled: YES! Brea thought they were regular pieces of wood, but she was wrong. Each dancer was holding a torch, and the square was lit up by these dancers twirling, spinning, dipping, and tossing pieces of wood into the square outlined in the sand. Once every torch was lit, the big lights went dimmer, and the torches became brighter. Between the dimmer lights and the fire from the torches, the costumes took on an illuminated and fierce appearance.

Regardless, Brea still thought this was insane. They continued to twirl and spin. To yell and chant. To dip and throw these little pieces of wood into a square in the sand. What was the point? Maybe this was why Ren and Tamron didn't want them to see because these people were crazy, and they were ashamed of anyone outside their Territory seeing this foolishness. The sun was beginning its descent, and as it did the people were yelling even louder. Is this how they celebrated their Ritual Day? With something that began during or after sunset? After asking herself those two questions, something else happened that changed her mind and attention. She heard the sound of screaming. Not the yelling of the crowd. These were blood curdling screams that sliced right through Brea's mind.

These were screams like she had never heard before, but the crowd was excited to a fever pitch upon hearing these horrifying sounds. Brea could not see where they were coming from. As much as she tried, the screaming was kept from her line of vision. The next thing that happened was the dancers and music stopped at the same time. The crowd fell silent, and all anyone could hear was the screaming from the unknown source.

The dancers closest to the beach parted to the left and right, and Brea could see a truck being driven into the square. There were two people in the truck, and the screaming was coming from the cargo inside the truck, but it was covered with black sheeting. The drivers stopped, got out, unhooked the front of the truck, and ripped away the black covering. Inside were Fodder! Black and Brown Fodder! The crowd went wild when they were revealed. The faces in the crowd that she could see were filled with hatred and disgust for the black and brown people caged in the box. The dancers at the opposite end of where the truck arrived parted to the left and right, and the two men got back into the truck driving the front of it away but left The Fodder in the box that fit perfectly into the square.

Brea was transfixed. She didn't want to observe anymore of this cruelty but was incapable of looking away. It didn't even occur to her to close the blinds. She felt trapped. A victim of her own decision that held her in a vice-like grip. The sun was lowering further, and the large lights were brightened so The Containers could see. The dancers closed the human square around this box of terrified and screaming people. Brea didn't care, anymore. Ren could call them Fodder all day long, but he was wrong! These were people. Men, women, and children. Why were The Containers scaring the wits out of them? What purpose did this serve? Brea got a fast answer to her wonderings.

The music and dancers started up again, and they twirled, spun, and dipped their torches toward the box of screaming black and brown people. This couldn't be happening thought Brea. This was too horrifying to believe. Was this torture or punishment for being caught by The Hunters? Is this what Ren meant by The Fodder being contained? To Brea, this was inhumane, and beyond the pale.

She felt rage growing inside of herself. She wanted to go out there and stop them, but how? There was only one of her, and what could she possibly do? A man appeared from behind the rock wall. He was gigantic!. He held a device in his hand, held it up to his mouth, and said: "Stop!" The dancing, music, and people all went mute except the people in the box. They kept screaming and crying, but the device the man held amplified his voice louder than their screams. He walked toward the box and began a speech.

"This is our Ritual Day. This is the day we come together every four months to celebrate our FREEDOM! And here they are before us. The ones that wanted to take our liberty and rights. The cursed ones. The infestation and cause of every ill and decay in our pursuit of happiness. They were subordinate for hundreds of years and kept in their proper place. We made a mistake 200 years ago and tried to view them as equal to ourselves. This never worked. It could never work because they are and will forever be inferior to us. No matter how hard we tried, they continually proved themselves to be incapable and beneath our contempt."

"As a wise man said over 210 years ago, this is the first place in the history of the world formed by the idea of Racial Supremacy, and we will never turn our back on those words again. The Fodder couldn't be happy and satisfied with being released from slavery, and still other kinds of Fodder wanted more than their due. They wanted more and more until we could not take their ineptitude and arrogance any longer. As one joined people, we gather here and do this."

Then the man lifted back his head, and reached his free hand up into the air and asked, "And we do this, why?"

Everyone in the crowd yelled together, "FOR OUR PLANET!"

The man laid down the device and joined the dancers for one full round of dancing and twirling around the box of screaming people. When he got back to his starting point, he picked up the device and was handed the largest torch she had ever laid eyes on! His torch made the others look like matchsticks. He began to speak once more.

"Glasses on!" said the enormous man.

Everyone put on a pair of glasses, but Brea didn't understand. The lights were on. The torches were lit. The sun that was setting wasn't going to make a difference in their ability to see.

The man took the huge torch and shoved it under the box. He then yelled into the device, "Why do we do this?"

"FOR OUR PLANET!" yelled the crowd.

Then the dancers took a step back, and he said it again and again. Each time the crowd yelled: "FOR OUR PLANET" they took a step back. This chanting and stepping backwards went on for about 20 paces. As the sunset was lowering into the ocean's horizon a blast of purple shot straight out of the box, and into the air! Though she was a fair distance away, she had to squint her eyes because of the intensity of the purple blast. The box was gone. The people in the box were gone, but not the purple. The purple went up, and then fanned out across the bluish black night sky.

Brea was dumbfounded for a minute, but found her voice, "My sunsets? My Sunsets! MY SUNSETS!?!"

And for the first time in her life, Brea fainted dead away.

Chapter Seventeen

Dillin had never fallen asleep. For the most part, he was keeping his eyes closed, but checking on Brea from time to time once she went to the window. He thought to himself how she couldn't help herself, not ever. When he opened his eyes and saw her on the floor, he sprung up to help her. Dillin did not take off his headset, but ran over to her, picked her up, and laid her on the couch. He put the puppy Brea had been playing with next to her and put a blanket over them both. He removed his headset. Dillin could hear whooping, shouting, and music, but he didn't hear anything that was alarming. He certainly didn't hear anything that was disturbing but refrained from looking out the window.

He began to gently shake her and said, "Brea, are you okay? Brea, answer me."

She was not responding, and he didn't know what to do for her. Dillin shook her shoulder a couple more times, but Brea wasn't waking up. He went to the bathroom and got a washcloth, drenched it in cold water, and laid it across her forehead with his good hand to try to rouse her. This was not working, either. Brea was not coming around, and he was at a total loss of what to do. Dillin sat down at the foot of the couch and kept stroking her arm and continued to whisper her name. He desperately wanted to help her, but it wasn't happening, and he became overpowered by feelings of helplessness.

After about thirty minutes had gone by, Brea began to moan. She was coming around, and Dillin was filled with relief. When she opened up her eyes, Brea saw Dillin but started screaming and screaming. Dillin grabbed Brea and held her. The pain in his arm was temporarily gone because of the adrenaline rushing through him from her screams and the petrified look in her eyes.

Dillin said, "Brea, It's okay. Honey, I'm here. It's okay."

She finally stopped screaming but started sobbing. Dillin kept holding onto her and repeated, "It's going to be alright. You'll see. Everything will be fine."

Finally, Brea said, "No. It's not okay. Nothing will ever be okay or fine."

Then she burst into tears once more, and Dillin just held her. He rocked her slowly back and forth in his arms and let her cry. He tried to lay her back down on the couch, but Brea grabbed onto him like he was life itself.

"Please! Please, don't leave me. Don't go. Don't go away!" said the hysterical girl.

"Brea, I'm not going anywhere. I won't leave you. It's okay."

"No. It isn't. What I saw was the most horrifying and terrible thing ever, and I can't pretend it wasn't," said Brea.

Dillin asked, "Why? Why did you have to watch?"

She whimpered and said, "Don't. Please, don't throw that in my face right now. I can't. I can't take it."

"I'm sorry. Brea, I'm sorry. I won't bring It up anymore," replied Dillin.

"I want you to take me to a bed, cover me up in blankets, and lay next to me. I can't stop shaking. I'm freezing," she said.

Dillin took her into one of the other bedrooms in Ren's house and laid next to her. Brea kept getting closer and closer to him. He gathered Brea up in his arms even though the pain was coming back, but she was shaking so hard. In a last effort to help, he enveloped his body completely around Brea, and she began to relax. This was a new sensation. He felt protective and somewhat aroused by her. This was not an appropriate time or place for any of this, but It was better than seeing his friend in such a state.

Whatever she saw, he was thankful he was spared the sounds and sights of it. Dillin held her until she cried herself back to sleep. Dillin didn't believe Ren would appreciate seeing them laying in one of his beds together for any reason, and carefully picked her up slowly and put her back down on the couch. About an hour later, Brea woke up. She was feeling nauseated and teary but much herself when Ren and Tamron returned to the house.

Ren spoke, "It's time. We have enough time to get you back to your boat and get you out of here."

The sound of Ren's voice had Brea leaping off the couch and her response was rapid and ferocious. "Rennet, how dare you?" she screamed and continued, "That is what you call saving The planet!?! Chanting together, FOR OUR PLANET while you do that!?! You lying, evil, rotten….."

She slapped Ren across the face, and then went for his throat with both hands. It was Tamron who ended this altercation and walked up behind Brea to shoot her in the arm with a needle. She went limp in Ren's embrace in mere seconds.

Dillin was up on his feet and said, "Hey! What have you done to her?"

Tamron replied, "We didn't know what we were walking into. We saw the blinds open and had to be prepared. What I shot Brea with will not harm her. It will just keep her asleep for about an hour. Did you both see?"

Dillin answered, "Only Brea, but what do you people do here?"

Ren replied, "You don't want to know. You don't ever want to know, and Brea shouldn't have found out, either. Now, let's get out of here!"

Tamron wrapped Brea up in a blanket and carried her. Ren and Dillin followed behind him, walking along the lanes of the rock walls until they came to the one hiding the boat they had arrived in.

Dillin said, "I don't know how you expect us to get home the way we came. We can't go up that raging water."

Ren turned around and said, "You can't go home the way you came, and you're not going to. Tamron and I will push your boat passed the breaking waves, and then you will start up the boat and keep going straight out to sea until it's flat. Then turn your boat right and keep parallel to the rock wall. After a while, you will notice a change in the air. It will not smell salty anymore.

Dillin asked, "It will smell like the lake?"

Ren replied, "Yeah, then you will know you are almost home. If I were you, I'd keep going for a while to avoid the rapids. This boat won't take another trip down the white water."

Dillin said, "Right. Got it."

As Tamron put Brea in the boat, Ren put in their packs and handed him a lantern.

Looking Dillin in the eye, Ren said many things, and ended with, "Please, tell Brea how sorry I am that she saw, and tell her she gave me a lot to think about."

"I will."

After a few seconds of thought, Ren added, "And tell her that I hope one day she can forgive me."

Dillin nodded in agreement, and there was nothing more to be discussed. He jumped into the boat, and the two young men pulled and pushed them out to sea beyond the big waves. Before he accelerated speed on the boat, Ren and Tamron waved goodbye with both calling out:

"Good Luck!" "Good Luck!"

The two of them turned away, swam to body surf a wave back towards shore, and they were gone.

Chapter Eighteen

Dillin reflected on the day and evening as Brea slept. It was one thing to be told about the old days by his Grandfather and quite another to learn the true circumstances about The Territory of The Containers. He knew that to be found out would mean catastrophe for their families. At the moment, his main concern was getting back home safely, but he was sure there would be obstacles. What would they be? He could not say, but simply continued to keep the boat parallel to the great rock wall.

Brea began to awaken. She looked at Dillin and said, "Where are we?"

"We're on our way home."

She began shaking, and Dillin put another blanket over her saying, "Please, try to stay calm."

Brea replied, "I don't know what Tamron shot in my arm, but I'm still pretty calm. I don't think I'll ever get over what happens there, and don't know how to deal with it."

"I'd prefer not knowing any part of it. After watching your reaction, I'll pass on the knowledge. Is that going to be a problem between us? I sound like a jerk, don't I?"

"No. Don't worry. Dillin, I won't tell you, and it certainly won't cause any friction between us. You were smart, but I wasn't," replied Brea.

"Ren had a message for you," said Dillin.

With her voice filled with venom, Brea said, "Dear Rennet! I don't want to hear any message from him. Not a word!"

"That's not fair to Ren or Tamron. They did protect and hide us. They fixed me up after I stole and wrecked Tamron's car. The two of them got us out of there, and told me how to get home," said Dillin and added, "They also gave us a choice and warned both of us. Sorry. I don't want to hurt you, but it's the truth."

She thought about Dillin's words in silence for a few minutes, and she knew that he was right. Brea also knew she owed Ren a lot of thanks for answering so many of her questions whether she liked the answers or not.

Brea relented, "Alright, give me the parting earful Ren has for me."

"He wanted me to say that even though you saw The Ritual that this was the part of his Territory that he, Tamron, and many others have a problem with accepting. He wanted me to say that he didn't partake in this, didn't like it, and would like it to end. That's why they would rather be anything but a person who takes part in The Ritual and picked for Containment Detail. He also said he was sorry you saw it, that you gave him a lot to think about, and hoped one day you could forgive him."

She laid there thinking about everything that had happened, and the many kindness's Ren had shown them. She thought about that beautiful ball of fur that kept her sane by simply laying in her lap. Her thoughts went to the full speed ride in his boat, and those beautiful blue Dolphins. They were magnificent to behold and be in their company. She had much to be grateful for as far as Ren was concerned.

The Ritual? She had to face the facts about that. It was her choice, and she made it of her own free will. She had no one to blame but herself. Underneath this night sky, she made peace with her decision. This was not Ren's fault, or anyone else's. It was hers, and she had to live with it by herself. She only hoped she would not go crazy in her mind by the searing images that she could not erase.

Brea sat up and said, "Yeah, watching is totally on me, and Ren was generous and kind to both of us."

"I Hope you can hold on to that. Brea, I hope you'll always remember that."

Soon the smell in the air began to change. They both knew the ocean was ending, and the lake was not far in the distance. Brea laid back looking at this wondrous night, and tried to take in the quiet, but her mind was wandering to the past. She thought to herself how many billions of people had died to make the planet clean and safe. How many more people were going to have to die to keep the planet that way?

It could never make sense in her mind because the world was, in fact, safe. But Brea did understand the power of ideas. She was aware how they could take root and make a lie reality. Her own delusions about becoming an Elite were proof enough. Her eyes had been opened. Brea could go back home, but she could never go back to not knowing. The truth had to be kept away even from her best friend, Dillin, who was her companion on this journey. It might not seem fair to carry the weight of the truth alone, but it was the right thing to do.

She didn't have a clue what she was going to do with this information internally. Facing this fact, her thoughts trailed off into her future. She did not want to be promoted. Absolutely not. She wanted her own ideas of freedom as false as they were. Up until now, she had felt free. This did not make sense, but she had felt free her entire life. Brea was certain that after a period of time she would continue to feel free, once more. In spite of everything, The Neighborhood was her home, and it always would be.

She didn't want to marry. The Elites might have her, but the prospect of parenthood was too boring for her to take seriously. She was aware that the teachers of the 4 to10-year-olds lived almost in a separate world of their own. Those teachers only had to state they had too much work to prepare, and they had a perfect excuse not to attend The Socials. Brea could be insulated from everything. Regardless of the temptation, Brea was an excellent Gamer, and she knew it. She would make an outstanding Assistant Coach and would do everything in her power to prepare younger students for their life with The Elites in her own way. This was her hope for herself.

While Brea looked up at the stars already regretting the vile words she said to Ren, she made a hope for him. She hoped his name was selected to be a Hunter. She hoped he didn't have to be a prisoner on that Space Station as a mechanic that housed all the trash and debris, and she knew without doubt Ren wouldn't handle it as a participant in The Ritual. She knew this about him in the deepest part of her heart. Tamron was included in her hope. They were fed different but similar lies from the beginning of their existence, too.

Ren and Tamron may have been told over and over that The Fodder weren't human, but they somehow knew better. Her heart went out to them, and she felt pity for their plight. When the mere thought of the black and brown people entered her mind, tears instantly filled her eyes. What was it that drove The Containers to participate in such heinous acts of destruction towards these people? How could a person not be a person because of their skin color? Brea couldn't comprehend any reasonable or rational answer to these questions. The speech by the massive man sounded like the most nonsensical gibberish she had ever heard in her lifetime.

She didn't even want to think about what would have happened to her or Dillin if those two wonderful young men had not found them before someone else had. Was that Good Fortune, or did they both get what Ren called: Lucky? As Brea and Dillin made their way around the great wall, they saw a faint light in the distance. When they got closer to land, a man was holding a lantern, and he was alone. They looked at each other with concerned faces but got out of the boat.

"I saw the two of you leave and have been waiting both days throughout the evening and until sunrise for your return," said the man.

Neither one of them knew if this was a good thing or a bad thing.

Chapter Nineteen

It has been 11 months since Brea and Dillin had returned from the land of The Containers. Eleven months since she had seen Ren. Brea spent a lot of time thinking about that day and night with him and contemplated much on one single word: Lucky. Brea thought she now knew what lucky meant. Brea did feel lucky to be home with her family. Lucky that she and Dillin had been found before sunrise by a lone man in the unknown Dining part of The Neighborhood. He brought them to an old, abandoned shack with a small room and bath, and there the two of them stayed for a couple of hours. He told them to use the shower inside.

"You both smell like the ocean, and that won't do," said the stranger. "Give me all your clothes, the backpacks, and I'll wash everything."

It took them a minute to notice the two large white robes in his hand, and they complied. Brea and Dillin took their showers and waited. The man came back with their belongings washed, and they both dressed into jeans with denim jackets. Dillin took off the bandages from his arm, and the injury didn't bleed. The deep cut only appeared to be a long scratch. Whatever that adhesive was that Tamron and Ren applied to his cut worked wonders and didn't leave a trace.

The stranger took the bandages, the two blankets Brea had been wrapped up in, Ren's old bodysuit, and the Container shirt Dillin had worn from that Territory and burned them in a circular pit outside. He told them he'd get them halfway home by way of a little cart and took them down along the side of the clear barrier. They had to weave around trees and bushes, but Brea and Dillin were full of appreciation for this man that seemed to come from nowhere to help them. If this wasn't lucky, she didn't understand the word one iota.

When he stopped the cart, he said, "You didn't meet me. I didn't see or come to your aid. Keep walking and say nothing about what you've discovered. And you better have the same story about what happened to you when you get home. Your safety depends upon these things."

Brea replied, "We understand. Thank you for your help."

The man nodded, turned his cart around, and went back on his way to the secret part of the Dining Neighborhood. Words were not needed between the teenagers for a while, but Brea's knee was starting to hurt. They stopped so she could rest, they both needed and drank some water, and came up with their story. The tale would be that they did discover different trees and bushes. They wandered away from the front of their homes, and lost track of the time. As they tried to make it back before dark, Brea tripped over a bush and hurt her knee to the point that she couldn't stand up. Dillin had tried to reach out and keep her from falling but fell with her and scratched his arm on the bush. There was no way Brea could go on, and they slept out there under the stars. Brea's knee was worse the next day, and they were happy to have brought some food and water with them. She was able to walk this morning, and they immediately started for home.

This was their story and they agreed not to vary from it. They kept on walking towards their houses and away from the barrier hoping to make it back. Brea and Dillin were hurting, hungry, and on the verge of collapse when one of their Gaming neighbors found them and brought them home. They were promptly scolded for taking off into the unknown, but their families and friends accepted their story and were delighted and relieved to see them again. Once in their houses, they were instantly instructed to sit in their chairs. Checking in was seen as the first important task these two had to do. It would keep The Healers from setting off any alarms. The bruises were iced, they were fed, and put to bed.

Lindy was thrilled to see her best friend, but Brea never took her into her confidence. She trusted Lindy absolutely but did not see a reason or purpose to scare her friend about The Containers, or The Elites. Another factor was complete adherence to the stranger who helped them and keeping themselves and their families safe. She and Dillin rarely communicated about their journey, and it was mostly done in whispers as they took walks down their street. Their parents would no longer allow them to go into the trees. The only things she missed, besides Ren, was the puppy she had played with and held onto for hours and memories of her ocean adventure. She had forgiven him long ago and felt deep sorrow that she couldn't take back the last words she had said to him in anger.

Dillin would speak mainly about his car ride, and she envied him. Dillin was incredibly lucky he had not seen The Ritual, but Brea had watched it in its entirety. That truth was something she could not talk to anyone about, and the recollections would appear in her mind without her permission or an appropriate outlet. Ren was correct that the actions taken did save the entire world, but to know of the suffering that brought it about and continued to this very day was incomprehensible. Why did it have to continue? How could it be stopped? Brea had no answers or power to change any of it, and she heard the words of her Grandma last season in her head:

"Sometimes, as the old saying goes, ignorance is bliss."

She wished she had listened to her Grandma's advice. She didn't and had to live with these horrible truths. So today, Brea wanted to be lucky just one last time. For again, it was Promotion Day in The Neighborhood. In the past, she had looked forward to this day with excitement, but today she felt only dread. She thought about Ren as she was getting ready, and hoped he was lucky, too. Brea smiled to herself when thinking about what a lousy Hunter he would make.

She also tried as hard as she could to forget about what Ren had told them both about the last four occupied houses in The Neighborhood. Brea knew that inside those houses, whose color stood for Erotica, were the young sex slaves being trained for The Elites. This disgusted her, and she felt lucky that she had not been born into that part of The Neighborhood. Most of all, Brea felt lucky that she was not viewed as Fodder, in this part of the world, simply because her skin was not white.

When the man strolled into the back door, Brea held her breath. She looked at him impassively but felt revulsion toward the man. At the end of the tryouts, he walked over to Coach Fernsbee, handed him the note and whispered to him. Brea's hope had not been in vain, and she was lucky. She was not promoted and took a seat in one of the ten chairs and waited. Lindy was promoted, and her face was filled with pure joy. Brea put a smile on her face for her friend and waved. Dillin was promoted too.

As their eyes locked, there was nothing they could say or do for one another. Dillin just turned and walked out with Lindy and the others that had been promoted and knew she wouldn't even be able to say goodbye to her two best friends. Her eyes brimmed slightly with tears for the loss of the one person who knew the truth about their day with The Containers. Coach Fernsbee saw this, but thought it was because she did not get promoted and ignored what he perceived as disappointment. He was correct, but wrong in his reasoning.

Brea sat and waited her turn to be called into the Coach's office. She had three options left to her: a parent, a teacher of the small children, or one of Coach Fernsbee's Assistants. She knew which one she would prefer, but it was not up to her. Brea heard her name called and went into the Coach's office. He wasted no time in letting her know her fate.

"I specifically asked for you to remain as an Assistant Coach," said Fernsbee.

"You did?" asked Brea.

"Yes. I know you perceive this as a failure considering your ranking, but I have an obligation to the future. In time, you could be Head Coach one day," he explained.

Brea did not want him to see how over the moon she was, and said in a monotone voice, "That would be a great honor. Thank you." She wrote her name on her assignment papers and left.

This was too good to be true! Never to leave her Neighborhood, never to leave her family, never to marry, and never to lay eyes on The Elites. Indeed, this was the luckiest day of her life! Time may not heal all wounds, but as it passed she became closer to her mom and brother. She formed new friendships with the other Assistant Coaches, and Brea still went to the third floor to visit her grandma in the evening. She didn't bring up what happened during those two days of her and Dillin's journey.

She felt thankful that she still had her Grandma, and that she possessed the Headgear to relive her youth in saving the world. After arriving home, Brea would not go onto the balcony. Her Grandma asked her about the sunsets only once and decided to drop the subject. She was incapable of viewing a sunset knowing what it truly signified. She was convicted and decided. Under no circumstance would Brea, on any account, witness another.

Printed in Great Britain
by Amazon